D1366987

Funny Money

Funny Money

TRACI DEPREE

GUIDEPOSTS
NEW YORK, NEW YORK

www.guideposts.com
(800) 431-2344
Guideposts Books & Inspirational Media

Cover design by Dugan Design Group
Cover illustration by Rose Lowry, www.illustrations.com
Interior design by Cris Kossow
Typeset by Nancy Tardi
Printed in the United States of America

For Amy Sue Hedden—
sister, friend, lover of children.

Chapter One

Jake Lourdes was always ill. Amy Lourdes, his mother, had told Kate Hanlon that he'd had a persistent cough practically from the time he was born.

Kate watched as the boy swung his skinny legs under the pew, his smiling face gazing adoringly at his father, who stood at the front of Faith Briar Church's sanctuary. Early June sunlight, diffused by a stained-glass window above the altar, filtered across the congregation that had become Kate's family in the small town of Copper Mill, Tennessee.

"When Pastor Hanlon told me that the church wanted to help with our medical expenses," Jake's father said, "well, I have to say I was humbled. As many of you know, we moved to Copper Mill a couple months ago. I work at the bank and am still learning my way around." He raised his brilliant blue eyes to scan the faces before him, then smiled, revealing his straight white teeth. "The people in Copper Mill have been so gracious to us." He smiled at his family.

His son gave him a little wave. Kate noted how the lines in Tim Lourdes' face softened when he winked at Jake.

"You see, our son Jake was born with cystic fibrosis," he went on. "I don't know how many of you know about CF. It's a genetic disorder that causes mucus buildup in the body. It affects all the organs, particularly the lungs and pancreas. That's why Jake always sounds like he has a cold—it's like chronic pneumonia. Plus, he has asthma, which is pretty common with CF."

Tim glanced down at his notes. Kate looked over at Amy Lourdes. The young mother held her six-year-old's small hand, stroking the back of it tenderly.

"The life expectancy for someone with CF," Tim went on, struggling with his emotions, "is in the thirties or forties, which is considerably higher than it used to be, because of new medical advances. Eventually Jake will most likely need a lung transplant, maybe have to go on dialysis or insulin. We're doing what we can to keep him healthy as long as possible." He paused as if the thought of such drastic measures was too painful to consider.

Kate felt her own eyes sting with unshed tears. How hard it must be for Tim and Amy to watch their child suffer from birth, knowing there was so little they could do to relieve it.

Paul Hanlon, Kate's husband and the pastor of Faith Briar, moved alongside Tim. Kate and Paul had been married almost thirty years, and she still enjoyed seeing him there at the front of the congregation, extending his kindness and wisdom to any who would hear.

"This has been a long, hard road for your family," Paul said as he placed a hand on the man's shoulders. "It takes a lot of courage to face what you face every day."

Paul turned to the congregation. "We believe the body of

Christ is called to serve those who struggle with illness, like Jake Lourdes. Matthew 25:36 says, 'I needed clothes and you clothed me, I was sick and you looked after me, I was in prison and you came to visit me.' These are the actions that tell the world we love God, more than any words we speak. If we show people his compassion, they'll see who Christ is in us."

Paul motioned to Jake and Amy to come forward. The six-year-old moved to stand next to his father, with Amy on the far side. He bit his lower lip and smiled shyly out at Kate before looking down.

"We're going to take a collection in a few minutes," Paul went on, "to help the Lourdeses with their many medical bills, but I also wanted to take this time to pray for Jake and his parents because we know that prayer accomplishes so much more than our own human strength. So if you'll all join me . . ."

Heads bowed as Paul began, "Father in heaven, you care about this struggling family more than we can possibly imagine. In the Bible you healed a lot of people, and you can heal Jake, but you are sovereign. You know what's best in the framework of eternity. Lord, help us as a church body to be sensitive to the needs of this family and all families that are hurting. Because that is what loving you is all about. You came to heal us in every way imaginable—physically, emotionally and spiritually. Work your will. We're trusting you. I ask that you help the Lourdeses with their many medical bills. We know that can put a strain on any family—on a marriage—so meet their needs, through our giving and through your many means, which are unfathomable to us."

The ushers moved forward to take the collection. When

the young family returned to their seats next to Kate, she saw tears streak down Amy's face.

Amy was a pretty young woman, in her late twenties, with pale blue eyes and straight dark brown hair that hung like a curtain. Kate had taken to her almost instantly. The love Amy felt for her son was evident in the looks she gave him, as was the strength of her connection to her husband.

Finally the ushers finished collecting the offering, and the organ burst forth with the doxology. Kate held the hymnal for the little boy, but he obviously didn't need it.

He sang loudly, enthusiastically, a child accustomed to intimacy with God.

"We can't thank you enough," Amy said to Kate and Paul as the congregation mingled after the service in the foyer. Jake had gone off to find his friends, and Tim had stayed behind in the sanctuary as others had gathered around him.

"If there's anything else you need," Kate said, "just let me know. We know how challenging it can be to move to a new town." She nodded to Paul, remembering their transition from Texas to Tennessee.

"I think we have everything unpacked." Amy smiled. "Finally. And Jake's made friends with the neighbor boy and some of the kids here at church. That's a huge relief." She glanced at her son across the way. "With all his hospitalizations and medical needs, I homeschool him, so making friends is his biggest hurdle."

"It must be hard for you too." Kate touched the young woman's arm.

"It can be. I've wanted to move home to Memphis for the longest time. There's an excellent cystic fibrosis hospital there, and my family's still there. But we've had a string of bad luck, so when Tim got this job in Copper Mill . . . well, it seemed to be God's answer to our prayers."

Kate nodded her understanding.

"I'm taking Jake to the T. C. Thompson Children's Hospital in Chattanooga tomorrow," Amy went on.

"Is there something new going on with him?" Paul asked.

Amy shook her head. "Not specifically, though with CF, there always seems to be something new. No, the doctors are talking about putting him on a new regimen of drugs for his asthma."

"That must be exhausting," Paul said.

Amy shrugged. "Unfortunately, you get used to hospitals after a while. Jake doesn't know anything else, so it isn't a big deal to him, though fitting in time for school can be tricky."

Just then, Tim came up to join their conversation.

"Where you been?" Amy said, smiling at him and caressing his arm.

"Chatting." He smiled.

The couple looked like models out of a fashion magazine, he with his blond Beach Boys look, and she, a dark-haired beauty.

"Can I ask you a personal question?" Kate said.

"How personal?" Tim said, teasing.

"Not too."

"Sure," Amy said.

"How did you two meet?" Kate asked.

Amy smiled up at her tall husband. "Tim was my tennis coach in college."

"Not really a coach," Tim corrected. "I taught private lessons to earn a few bucks, and Amy was trying to pass her phys-ed requirement—she was pathetic." He quirked a brow.

"That didn't stop you from asking me out," Amy retorted.

"I knew if I didn't, you'd never improve that serve." They laughed.

"Do you still play tennis?" Paul asked.

"Not so much anymore," Tim said. "Once Jake came, he kind of filled up our lives."

"Children do that, sick or not," Kate said.

Jake's cough could be heard amid the laughter of his peers across the small foyer.

"We wouldn't have it any other way," Amy said.

Just then, Joe Tucker, a Faith Briar regular, came up. He walked with a cane and a bit of a limp. Tufts of white hair that fringed his mostly bald head stuck out from the back, refusing to be orderly. The elderly man held out a hand to Tim Lourdes.

"I have to shake your hand, young man," he said.

"Really?" Tim took the older man's hand.

"I appreciate what you said up there this morning." He paused before going on. "You see, my niece's little girl had CF too. It was a cruel, cruel thing . . ." His words fell away. Finally he shook his head. "Well, I just wanted you and your wife to know that we at Faith Briar are glad you're here. Anything we can do to make things easier, well, don't be afraid to ask."

Chapter Two

"The deposit can wait until Millie gets back from vacation on Friday," Paul said of the church secretary the next morning as he finished shaving.

Kate leaned against the door frame, a cup of steaming coffee in her hands. She'd just come from her favorite chair after her morning prayer and Bible reading. Young Jake Lourdes had been heavy on her mind.

"There's no reason to wait," Kate assured. "Besides, Millie asked me to take care of it, and I'm sure Amy and Tim could use the extra money right away."

"Would you like to write the church newsletter while you're at it?"

"Are you serious?"

"No." He smirked.

Kate swatted him playfully as he scooted past her into the hallway.

"And, honey . . ." Kate leaned close to his clean-shaven face, which smelled of soap.

"What?" He turned to look at her.

She kissed his cheek. "That's all," she said with a wink.

PAUL OPENED the church safe where each Sunday's deposit was kept for Millie Lovelace to process each Monday. He set a large manila envelope as well as a smaller envelope marked "Lourdes" on Millie's desk.

Soon Kate was immersed in numbers, first counting out the loose cash, then recording each gift on the computer. Not all the donations were in marked envelopes; some cash gifts were in unmarked envelopes as well.

Once she'd finished the general collection, Kate turned to the gifts for the Lourdes family in the second envelope. Since these were designated for an individual family and not for the church, Kate could simply add up the monies without all the tax-regulated rigmarole.

She was halfway through counting when she noticed a plain white business-sized envelope with "Tim Lourdes" scrawled in cursive across its front. It lay on top of Millie's stack of in-box items with a Post-it note that read, "Don't forget: twenties and fifties," in a slanted handwriting. Kate reached for it, wondering if it was another gift meant for the needy family. It wasn't sealed, so she looked inside. There was cash in it, with a second note that read, "Add to the Lourdes' gifts on Sunday."

Kate added the cash to her pile and continued counting. All told, there was more than three hundred dollars for the Lourdes family, a very generous gift for a church the size of Faith Briar.

Kate began to count the money a second time to make

sure she hadn't miscalculated. Halfway through, however, one of the bills caught her attention. There was something odd about it; the color wasn't quite the same as the other bills—it was a little bluer than it should have been. She held it up to the light. Maybe it was the fluorescent fixtures creating the illusion. She studied it closer.

No. It still didn't seem quite right. She took it to the window and opened the blinds. Morning sunlight streamed in. Kate looked at the bill again and pulled several other bills from the regular collection to compare them. Sure enough, the color of the twenty-dollar bill was noticeably bluer than the bill of the same denomination from the offertory. When she studied it closer, she saw that Jackson's image seemed slightly blurry. Hardly a perfect forgery, but good enough to fool someone who didn't have the time to examine it.

"Paul . . . ," she called.

"What is it?" His voice sounded distracted in the next room.

"Can you come here?"

She riffled through the other bills on the desk, studying each closely. Sure enough, there were several other bills with the same bluish hue in the stack.

"What are you doing?" Paul studied her as he came alongside the desk.

"Take a look at these." Kate held the questionable money out for him to examine. After giving her a curious look, he took the first bill and bent his head to study it.

Finally he lifted his head. "What's the problem?"

"Does it look right to you?"

"Why? Do you think it might be counterfeit?"

Kate nodded.

"It *feels* like real money." He rubbed his thumb and forefinger across the surface, then he wadded up the bill and flattened it out, even giving it a snap at the end to demonstrate its clothlike properties.

"But look at the printing"—she handed him the bill she'd taken from the regular offering—"and compare it to this."

"They do look different," he said as he examined to see if it had the magnetic strip. It did.

"There are several others." Kate held up the other bills. "Fifty dollars' worth."

"So, what do we do?"

"We call the sheriff."

IN THE TIME it took Sheriff Roberts to arrive in his black-and-white SUV, Kate had looked through the general donations again to see if she'd missed any fake bills in there. All of the counterfeits were in the offering for the Lourdes family.

Alan Roberts was now bent over the desk studying the currency notes as Paul had done earlier, using a magnifying glass for closer inspection. After a long silence, he lifted his head.

"Do you know who put this in the plate?"

Kate shook her head. "It was part of a special offering."

"And that was for . . . ?"

"To help Amy and Tim Lourdes. They have a son with cystic fibrosis."

"Isn't Tim the new loan officer at the bank?"

Kate nodded.

The sheriff's brow puckered, and he gave the bill another

perusal before placing it in a plastic evidence bag and removing the latex gloves he'd put on earlier.

"I'm assuming these will have your prints all over them?"

"Probably," Kate said. "Both Paul and I handled the bills."

"We'll need to get you fingerprinted, then, if you can stop by the deputy's office later today. It's routine, so we can rule out your prints and distinguish them from the counterfeiter's."

Both nodded that they would.

"So," Paul began, "these *are* counterfeit?"

"I'm afraid so." He eyed the plastic bag. "I'm going to need a record of everyone who was in attendance. Do you have something like that?"

"Sure," Paul offered, "We have attendance sheets that most everyone signs. We can get you those later today."

The sheriff nodded, though his expression clouded.

"To be honest," he said, "there have been other bills passed in town. But with these bills . . ." He looked away and sighed. "Apparently our counterfeiter attends Faith Briar Church."

Chapter Three

The counterfeiter was one of their own?

Kate couldn't get Sheriff Roberts' comment out of her thoughts. Who among their faithful would do such a thing—and then add insult to injury by putting the phony bills in the offering plate for the needy family? It didn't make sense.

As soon as Sheriff Roberts left, Kate pulled up the list of declared donations she'd just entered into Millie's computer. She printed off two copies, then took the sheets from the attendance pads and typed up an additional list of those who'd been in attendance the previous morning. She'd drop both at the deputy's office later in the day when she and Paul stopped in to have their fingerprints taken.

"Ready?" Paul asked, coming up behind her.

Kate gathered the sheets from the printer and tucked them into a folder. She turned to meet her husband's gaze.

"Who would do this?" she said.

Paul shook his head. "It's hard to say. Someone who's desperate for an easy buck, I guess."

IT WAS ONE O'CLOCK by the time Kate and Paul made it to the Country Diner for lunch, after stopping by the deputy's office. It was often their habit to head to the local eatery, where folks gathered for a grilled cheese on rye, a strong cup of coffee and neighborly chatter.

They'd made plans to meet Livvy and Danny Jenner there since their teenage sons were away at summer camp for the week. Danny waved them over.

In his late forties, Danny was tall and slender with curly dark hair. As head of the church board, he spent a lot of time with Paul discussing church business. Livvy was also in her late forties, though with her short auburn hair, high cheekbones, and hazel eyes, the town librarian looked much younger.

Paul slid into the blue vinyl booth next to Danny, while Kate took the seat next to Livvy.

"You look troubled," Livvy said.

Kate blew out a breath. "It's been quite a morning." She laughed, releasing some of the tension that had built up in her body.

"Everything okay?" Danny turned to Paul.

Paul began, "Kate was doing the deposit this morning at church, and"—he shook his head—"there were counterfeit bills in the offering for the Lourdes."

"Counterfeits?" Danny and Livvy said together, puzzled expressions on both their faces.

"Did you call the sheriff?" Danny said.

Kate nodded and explained everything that Sheriff Roberts had said. She finished by saying, "The sheriff suspects that someone from Faith Briar is a counterfeiter."

Kate felt betrayed, hurt by the very idea. Paul reached across the table to take her hand.

"I can't picture anyone from our church doing this." Livvy's words echoed Kate's thoughts. "You have no idea who it could be?"

Paul shook his head.

LuAnne Matthews came by the table. The heavyset waitress was in her early fifties. Freckles danced across her ruddy face and her green eyes still sparked with mischief. She was a fixture at the Country Diner, always ready with a smile and friendly conversation. She looked through horn-rimmed glasses at them.

"Hey, y'all," she said. Her polyester dress and a no-nonsense white apron made her look like she had stepped right out of the 1950s. "We've got a delicious special today—grilled pear-and-ham sandwich with cilantro and homemade fries."

"Grilled pears?" Danny said with a shiver.

"Might not sound good, but it tastes amazing," LuAnne said.

"I'll try that," Kate said.

The rest of the group ordered, then Livvy returned to their conversation.

"So what are they going to do about this counterfeiter?"

"The sheriff is calling the Secret Service, I guess. Counterfeiting is a federal crime," Paul said.

Livvy's expression was troubled. "It's just . . . wrong," the librarian said. "I understand *buying* stuff with counterfeit money—at least that makes sense in a twisted kind of way. But to put it in an offering? I don't get it. That poor family." She sighed.

Kate reached into her handbag and pulled out the digital camera she'd brought along to the service the day before. She'd taken a photo of the Lourdes family for the bulletin board in the foyer of the church to remind congregants to pray. She found the shot and showed it to Livvy.

"That's a great picture of the family," Livvy said.

Jake grinned between his parents, so proud and energetic.

Kate nodded and tucked the camera back into her handbag. "Paul and I had a long talk with Tim and Amy," she said. "They've really been through a lot with Jake. He's had several lung infections that they thought might be terminal."

"Yet they keep moving forward." Livvy shook her head. "It breaks my heart."

It was no wonder Livvy had become her dear friend since she and Paul moved to Copper Mill. The woman cared deeply for others.

"So on a lighter note, are you going to join me in my torture?" Danny turned the attention to Paul.

"Huh?" Paul looked over at Livvy, who had a grin on her face.

"I just talked Danny into taking ballroom dance lessons with me." She raised an eyebrow and nodded from Kate to Paul.

"I don't know if Paul loves me *that* much," Kate teased. She gave his hand a squeeze.

"Oh brother." Paul reached for the glass of water LuAnne had placed in front of him and took a sip.

"He's dodging," Kate whispered. "Fear of dancing."

"Come on, Paul," Livvy said. "Don't you think it'd be fun?"

Kate had heard about the new studio in town called

Classical Ballroom that had opened up on Sweetwater Street, but other than a few wedding dances in their younger days, she and Paul hadn't done a whole lot in the world of the waltz or the cha-cha. Paul was too humble to admit that he was as good as he actually was. Kate pictured Paul gliding across a polished floor.

"The woman who teaches at Classical Ballroom stopped in at the library a few days ago," Livvy went on, "and dropped off a few brochures. They're offering six-week sessions with two classes per week. It isn't a long-term commitment. If it really isn't your thing, you don't have to sign up for another session . . ."

"Hal and Audrey Harper are the owners, right?" Paul said. "Weren't they at church a few weeks ago?"

"I met them," Kate said. "They moved to town a couple months ago. He's retired, and she runs the studio."

"Oh, to be in my fifties and retired," Danny said with a smile. "I obviously chose the wrong career."

"I'd hardly call running your own dance studio *retired*," Livvy said. "He's as active in it as she is. They compete too. Audrey said they were going to be out of town at competitions all weekend."

Kate turned to Paul. "It wouldn't be a long-term commitment." She repeated what Livvy had said, not wanting to sound as if she was begging, though she knew she did.

"All right," Paul grimaced. "But let it be noted that I officially do love you enough to look ridiculous in public."

Chapter Four

Paul returned to the office after dropping Kate at home. The house was quiet, save for the hum of the ancient refrigerator in the kitchen. Kate kept replaying the morning's events in her mind. A counterfeiter? At Faith Briar Church?

Who would betray them like that? Kate pulled out a stool at the kitchen counter, took a seat, then lowered her face into her hands. A prayer rose from her lips, unbidden. "Father, please help us understand what's going on here. What's *really* going on. Why would someone make counterfeit money and put Faith Briar Church right in the middle of their treachery?"

A verse came to her, from Proverbs. She got up and found the passage in her Bible. "Some who are poor," she read into the quiet, "pretend to be rich; others who are rich pretend to be poor." Wasn't that exactly what this person was trying to do? Pretend? She bowed her head again and added, "Lord, we all pretend in one way or another, but you shine your truth on our pretenses and show us who we really are in you. Please do that here."

Calm filled her. Prayer had a way of changing her as she talked to God.

She reached for the papers she'd printed at the church office. She'd made extra copies for herself and promised Sheriff Roberts that she'd let him know if she found anything unusual.

Kate cross-checked the attendance list and the donations list. If the person's name was on the offering list, she placed a mark in front of each name on the attendance sheet. This way she could tell who had attended, who didn't give or who gave anonymously. The problem was, with a special offering, it wasn't uncommon for someone who had written a check for the general offering to pull out cash for the second offering. But at least it was something to start with.

There were two names without marks. Kate studied them closely. The first was Abby Pippins, a friend and local ceramics artist. Kate couldn't imagine the sweet woman being a counterfeiter. The second name on the list was J. B. Packer, the part-time fry cook at the Country Diner.

It wasn't much to go on—the fact that the two hadn't written their names on their offering envelopes or perhaps they hadn't added anything to the offering that morning—but at least she could ask them questions, see if there was anything to her assumption that a counterfeiter wouldn't announce his—or her—crime by writing his or her name down. If there was nothing to it, she could at least ask them if they'd seen anything suspicious during the service.

Kate sighed, yet the calm she felt from her prayer remained. She tucked the handwritten list in her handbag.

She didn't have any idea who was behind this, but it was a starting point.

KATE VISITED ABBY FIRST. She wanted more than anything to clear Abby's and J.B.'s names as soon as possible. These were people she cared about, not swindlers. Or were they? Kate shook her head.

Abby lived in a tiny one-story on Sweetwater. Flowerpots on the front porch were bursting with early summer blooms, and two old rockers swayed slightly with the breeze as she drove up. Kate knocked on Abby's screen door. The inner door was wide open, and the smell of something burning from out back bit Kate's nose.

"Abby?" she called out.

"Hi, Kate." The woman bustled down the hall. "I was out back and didn't hear you." Her smile lit up her round face like a jack-o'-lantern.

She opened the screen door to let Kate in. "I'm firing some pots," she explained as she pinched her nose. "This glaze I'm using is particularly stinky."

She led the way to the kitchen at the back of the house and turned on the water in the sink. "Sorry, my hands are all dirty." She scrubbed them clean, then flicked the water off and reached for a towel from the handle of the stove. "One of the hazards of the job. So"—Abby looked Kate in the eye—"can I interest you in some iced tea?"

"Oh," Kate said, "I don't want to impose."

Abby waved a hand as if she were batting a fly. "It's no imposition." She opened a small refrigerator and pulled out a frosty pitcher of iced tea with lemon slices floating on top. She poured two cups, handing one to Kate, then she led the way to a patio out the back door.

"It's such a glorious day," Abby said over her shoulder. "It's a shame to waste it inside."

The back patio was a cottage garden with flowers planted here and there, amid paths of stone and moss, statues and fountains. Abby pulled out a black wrought-iron chair for Kate at a round table with a lantern at its center, then tugged out another for herself.

"So"—she smiled at Kate—"what's on your mind?"

Kate inhaled the scent of sage, not sure how to begin.

"We had a bit of a disturbance this morning," she said slowly. She wanted to choose her words carefully. "There were counterfeit bills in yesterday's offering."

"Oh my! That's awful!" Abby covered her mouth with her hand. "Who would have done that?"

Kate shook her head. "Well . . . I was hoping you might help me figure that out."

"Me?" Abby pointed to herself, incredulous.

"Did you by any chance see anything unusual? Maybe there was someone new in church?"

Abby shook her head. "Nothing that comes to mind . . . Wait. There was a man in the foyer, now that I think about it. It was right before church started. I thought he'd take a seat, but then he left. Seemed odd to me that he'd come but then not attend."

"What did he look like?" Kate leaned forward.

"I didn't get a good look at him, but I noticed him because

he wore penny loafers without socks." She chuckled. "I never understood how people could do that."

"Was he alone?" Kate took a sip of her tea and watched Abby over the rim of her glass.

"Far as I could tell, but he probably wouldn't have been there when the offering was taken."

"Thanks, Abby." Kate set down her glass and nodded. "That helps."

As Kate looked at Abby, she knew the woman was no counterfeiter. Counterfeiters were false, filled with pretense. Abby Pippins was nothing if not genuine.

J. B. PACKER had mostly kept to himself since the deaths of his wife and daughter, though Kate did see him working from time to time at the Country Diner. He came to church now and then, and J.B. had signed the friendship pad at Faith Briar the day before. He must've snuck out of church, though, because she hadn't seen him after the service.

Kate found him in the parking lot out in the back of the Country Diner. A tall hedge gave the lot privacy, and she knew J.B. often came here on his breaks to get some fresh air. A large Dumpster sat along its perimeter. It smelled of refuse and old food.

Middle-aged, J.B. had thin, grayish brown, collar-length hair. Dark circles ringed his eyes when he lifted them to Kate. He stepped back, obviously surprised by her presence.

"Oh, Mrs. Hanlon," he said, shoving his hands into his pockets. "I didn't see you there."

"How are you, J.B.?" Kate asked.

The man shrugged. "Fair to middlin'," he said. "I get by."

Kate smiled. "Say, I noticed from the friendship pad that you were at church yesterday."

"I get a personal visit for that?" He laughed.

Kate chuckled with him, and she saw his crow's-feet crinkle. He was a smart man. He'd even been valedictorian of his graduating high school class, but as happened to so many, a few poor choices and more than a few losses in life had beaten him back. But still, looking at his wide eyes, Kate was convinced that like Abby, he couldn't be the counterfeiter. He'd been through a lot, but that didn't make him a criminal.

"Did you enjoy the service?" Kate asked.

He shrugged. "Wasn't bad." His eyes clouded, and he shook his head. "Needed some time away from my place," he admitted.

Kate touched his arm, concerned about him. "Troubles?" she asked simply.

"No more than anyone else's troubles, Mrs. Hanlon."

"That doesn't make them any easier to bear though." Kate wanted to help him but wasn't sure how.

"Bein' there yesterday helped some," he admitted. He looked away. "I appreciate your concern, though."

"We're here for you. You know that, right?"

His lips pursed together. "Well, I need to get back or Loretta will come lookin' for me." He gave a two-finger salute. "Thanks."

Then he disappeared inside the back door, and Kate watched it closely. She hadn't asked him any questions about the counterfeit money, but then she hadn't needed to.

Chapter Five

The phone rang at the Hanlon house after Kate had returned from running her errands on Tuesday. She knew the gossip circle was already in full swing.

"What happened at church Sunday?" Renee Lambert demanded when Kate answered.

"What are you talking about?"

"A couple of *suits* are running around town asking people about counterfeit money passed at the church."

Kate could hear Renee's dog, Kisses, barking in the background.

"Suits?"

"Yes, the Secret Service. So what happened?"

Kate hesitated, then finally told Renee about the bills she'd found in the special offering. She knew the woman well enough to know that no juicy tidbit went unexplored on her watch.

"So who could it be?" Renee said in a conspiratorial tone.

"I don't know. That's for the Secret Service to discover," Kate said. She wouldn't admit it to Renee, but the thought that the counterfeiter was someone from their own midst meant they wouldn't be the only ones looking into it.

THE TWO AGENTS accompanied Sheriff Roberts to the parsonage at two o'clock that afternoon. Kate heard their insistent knock on the front door before she saw their dark-colored vehicle parked in the driveway just behind the sheriff's SUV.

Kate had been in her stained-glass studio working on a set of windows for an antique china cupboard, a special Internet order for a woman from Pine Ridge. Taking off her apron and stopping to wash her hands in the bathroom, she walked quickly to the door as the pounding continued.

She opened the door with a smile. "Sorry about the delay. You caught me working."

Sheriff Roberts nodded, then tilted his head to the two men who stood on each side of him.

"These two gentlemen are with the Secret Service," he began. "They're in town about the counterfeiting scam."

Kate shook hands with each and motioned for them to come inside.

"I'm glad to help however I can," she said as they took seats in the tan slip-covered sofa in Kate's spacious living room. Kate opted for the rocking chair.

The one on the right reminded Kate of a taller Tom Cruise, with blond hair, blue eyes and a slight crook to his nose as if he'd been punched one too many times. The other was a portly, round-faced man who looked to be in his mid- to late fifties, with glasses perched on the end of his nose and a bald head. Not a speck of hair remained on its shiny surface.

"This is Agent Norris," the sheriff pointed first to the Tom Cruise look-alike, then to the bald man, "and Agent Wimper."

Agent Wimper pulled out a pad of paper and a pen while Agent Norris leaned toward Kate in an interrogative pose.

"Mrs. Hanlon, can you tell us everything that happened, everything you saw?" he said. "And start at the beginning."

"The beginning?" Kate said with a glance at Sheriff Roberts.

"Yes." Wimper cleared his throat and ran a hand atop his shiny head. "We have it here that you were the one who detected the bills at Faith Briar Church . . ."

"Yes, sir," Kate said.

"So it says in the report that you were working at the church . . . doing the deposit?" He looked at her over the top of his glasses.

"Yes," Kate said. "I was getting it ready for the bank. But the counterfeits were in the offering for the Lourdeses."

"This is Tim and Amy Lourdes?" She was surprised they'd heard about the family already.

Kate nodded. "We took a special offering for their son, Jake. He has cystic fibrosis."

The men didn't say anything.

The bald one looked back at his notes.

"Now"—he cleared his throat—"tell us how you discovered the bills."

"As I said, I was doing the deposit for the Lourdeses, and I noticed that some of the bills looked bluer than the rest, and the printing seemed a little blurry. When I compared them to some other bills, I thought we might have been dealing with counterfeits. That's when I looked through the rest and found the other bills. There weren't any in the general offering."

"Are there any church members who you think would do something like this?" Agent Norris asked.

"I've given that a lot of thought," Kate admitted, then shook her head, "but I can't think of anyone. Abby Pippins did mention seeing a strange man at church, but I don't know . . ."

Agent Norris studied her for a moment. "Did she give a description?"

"Not really," Kate admitted. "Just that he was wearing loafers without socks. And she said he was gone by the time the offering was taken. I can't imagine who it could be."

"There wasn't anything strange about the service?" the agent pressed.

"Well, there was also an envelope," Kate said. "It was left on Millie's desk with Tim Lourdes' name on it."

"You mentioned this when Sheriff Roberts came by?" Agent Wimper asked. He turned to the sheriff, who confirmed with a nod that she had.

"Do you know how it came to be on the secretary's desk?" Norris asked.

"No. It was just there when I went in," Kate said.

"Do you know if the counterfeit bills came from that envelope?" Agent Wimper wiped his head, now damp with sweat, with a handkerchief.

"It was cash, no name on it or anything, just a handwritten note, so I mixed it with the rest of the donations. The bills could've been from there, but there's no way to know."

"Do you have the envelope?"

"I took it as evidence yesterday when I first questioned Mrs. Hanlon," Sheriff Roberts interjected.

Norris jumped in. "Do you know where we can reach the church secretary?"

"Millie Lovelace," Kate clarified. "She's on vacation."

"And did she tell you where she was going?"

"No, but you could ask my husband. I don't have a lot of interaction with Millie; I mean I don't work with her like he does. He's at the church."

"All right. We'll head there next."

The men stood to go. Wimper tucked the notepad and pen back into his briefcase, then reached to shake Kate's hand. "We appreciate all your help on this. If you think of something else or anything comes back to you, please let us know."

The other agent handed her a card with his contact information on it and nodded his thanks before the two headed out the door. The sheriff followed behind but paused at the door and looked at Kate.

"Agent Norris has cracked a lot of these cases," he said, "so I believe we can trust him to find out who did this." He tipped his officer's hat to her before walking out the door.

WHEN PAUL CAME HOME at three for a late lunch, he looked as puzzled as Kate had felt after her visit from the Secret Service.

"So the Secret Service found you too?" she said as she set a steaming bowl of chicken chow mein on the table.

"How can you tell?"

"Your overwhelmed expression." She smiled at him, and Paul leaned over to give her a peck on the cheek before heading to wash his hands at the kitchen sink.

"They asked some odd questions, that's for sure," he said once he'd turned off the water.

"Like what?"

Paul dried his hands on a towel and took his seat at the oak dining table. "A lot of questions about Millie."

"They asked me about Millie too." Kate reached for his hands, and the two bent their heads in prayer before digging in.

"They were pretty probing," Paul went on. "As if they think Millie's a suspect."

"Did they say she was a suspect?" Kate furrowed her brow.

"No. But they were definitely digging for something." He took a bite of the steaming dish and closed his eyes in satisfaction. "I love your chow mein. You should make it more often." Paul winked at her and took another bite.

"They'll rule her out quickly," Paul went on. "Millie's hardly savvy with technical stuff. Printing money? There's no way she'd be our counterfeiter."

Kate agreed with Paul. After all, Millie still used the paper calendar on her desk to keep track of Paul's schedule. And yet . . . Kate thought about the Post-it note that had said, "Don't forget: twenties and fifties." Maybe there had been more to that note than she'd first thought.

"Maybe they aren't thinking she'd be the one to create the bills . . . just that she'd use them?" Kate speculated, as much to herself as to Paul. She took another mouthful of her food. "What about her husband?"

"Boom? He's come by the office a few times," Paul said. "He's a hardworking guy. Blue collar and honest."

"So who do you think it could be?" Kate asked.

"Could be anyone."

"Anyone from Faith Briar, you mean," Kate said with a frown. "This is *our* church, Paul. I keep thinking about all of our members, and there isn't one I can identify who would do something like this."

Paul's tender gaze met hers. "The guilty party will be found, Katie. Whether it's a member of Faith Briar or from somewhere else."

"I know." She laid down her fork. "But I hate to think that someone we trust could be deceiving us."

Chapter Six

Agent Wimper called a town meeting Tuesday night. Every business owner and retailer had been personally invited to the event at Copper Mill Public Library's meeting room. Even the local churches had been called to attend.

When Kate and Paul arrived five minutes before the meeting was due to begin, the chairs in the room were almost all taken. The large table that usually occupied the center had been replaced by folding chairs, and an overhead projector and screen had been set up. Familiar faces and loud chatter filled the room.

Betty Anderson of Betty's Beauty Parlor waved for Kate and Paul to sit beside her, so they made their way over to where Betty and her husband Bob sat. Betty had short bleached-blonde hair and a penchant for chatter, while Bob was a quiet man who chose his words carefully.

"Isn't this exciting?" Betty said, leaning toward Kate, her face alight.

Kate glanced at the front, where a dark-suited Agent Wimper stood with arms crossed, looking forbidding. She got the sense that if anyone made a wrong move, he would be on them like flies on watermelon. She didn't see Agent Norris anywhere. Glancing around, she saw Sam Gorman, the owner of the Mercantile; Emma Blount from the ice-cream shop; the Cline sisters from the bank; Eli Weston of Weston's Antiques; and many other familiar faces.

Finally, the bald, portly agent moved to the podium that was set up at the front of the room. He tapped the mic to be sure it was on.

"If all of you will take your seats, please," he said.

The crowd quieted.

"I'm Secret Service Agent Wimper. I've called you all here to inform you of what's going on, though I'm sure most of you know already. I'll also educate you on what to be on the lookout for. Several counterfeit bills have shown up in Copper Mill, at Faith Briar Church as well as several businesses in town."

Murmurs spread through the crowd, and Agent Wimper held up a hand to quiet everyone. "You all are our best allies in catching the criminal, so we're here to talk about what to look for and what to do if you suspect someone of trying to pass off fake money at your business or church."

He said church meaningfully and looked directly at Kate. Her thoughts went straight to Millie and that envelope. His insinuation was clear. But Agent Wimper paused as he reached into a big portfolio on a narrow table beside him.

"This"—he held up a bill—"is a counterfeit five-dollar bill. All of the bills we've found so far are dated pre-1996. Of course, they were actually printed much more recently than that." He handed the bill to Steve Smith of Smith Street Gifts. "You can pass that around," he said, then turned his attention back to the full room.

"As you'll see, these notes look very similar to real money. This counterfeiter has found a way to make his, or her, money *feel* like real money. That makes him harder to catch. He's smart. The main things to look for are variations in ink color and a blurry register, when the lines aren't crisp looking. Real money is particular and exacting. This fake stuff tends to look a bit strange because home-based scanners and printers simply can't handle that level of detail."

He then turned to the overhead projector set up alongside the lectern and further illustrated the difference between real and phony currency. When he was done, he pulled out a yellow pen and held it up.

"We're going to pass these out to everyone." He handed a box of the pens to go around the room. "These are counterfeit checking pens; use them at your checkout lanes. The ink in them reacts to the ink in real bills, so it makes detecting fakes much easier."

He demonstrated by drawing a short line on a real twenty-dollar bill. The ink turned a faint brown. "If this had been a fake bill, the ink would have turned dark brown or black. If you know of anyone in the community who isn't here and who needs a pen, please feel free to take them some." He waited while the box of pens was passed around the room. "I've got business cards here so you can call me or my partner, Agent Norris, who couldn't make it tonight."

Finally he opened the discussion to questions. He pointed to someone near the back of the room.

"Do you think whoever it is might be acting alone or do they have accomplices?" Kate didn't recognize the voice.

"With the number of places the bills have been passed, the sheer quantity of bills and the various methods of manufacture," he said, "we suspect there is more than one person involved."

Then he lifted his gaze to meet Kate's and Paul's. "Based on where the bills are showing up, we feel certain that they're coming from somewhere in Copper Mill. None have surfaced, at least yet, in Pine Ridge or any other neighboring town. We want to keep it that way."

A woman raised her hand in front of Kate. She had gray hair that frizzed off the top of her head and a high voice. Kate recognized her as Audrey, the dance instructor she had met at church.

"How do we know we aren't accidentally passing the money ourselves? Will we be arrested too?"

The agent shook his head. "First of all, if you look for the things we've talked about here"—he motioned toward the overhead projector and then toward the pens—"you'll be able to spot most of the fakes for yourself. It really shouldn't be a concern. If money does happen to get passed, we will of course want to talk to you. It is a crime to knowingly pass counterfeit money, but it's manufacturing it that will put someone behind bars for a very long time."

WEDNESDAY AFTERNOON, Kate made her way to the new dance studio that Livvy had told her about. The name

Classical Ballroom swung above the door on a wooden sign held aloft on a horizontal flagpole. It flapped back and forth with the breeze.

Inside was a warm-looking room with mirrors on three sides and a wall of windows looking out over Sweetwater Street on the fourth. The mirrors made the room appear larger than it was, which was no more than thirty feet by thirty feet. Hardwood floors with a cherry finish shone in the reflection. The lone piece of furniture in the room was a beat-up desk where a receptionist would sit, an old church pew near the door and a piano with a matching bench on the opposite side. The only thing that broke up the expanse of mirrors was a horizontal dance bar that ran the length of one wall.

Kate took note of her reflection. She wore a sharp pink and orange paisley top with a pencil skirt that complemented her mature yet trim figure. Her medium-length strawberry blonde hair was cut in a bob and tucked behind her ears.

"Hello," Kate called into the quiet. She didn't see anyone about. She moved into the room and when nobody appeared, she turned around, ready to leave, when the sound of someone bustling in a back area halted her.

"Can I help you?" a tall woman said as she entered the room from a hallway to the left. It was Audrey, the instructor. Her frizzy gray hair darted from her head like an exploded bird's nest. Her eyes were as pale and bright as robin's eggs, which when Kate considered her hair, seemed appropriate.

"I was sorting through some paperwork," Audrey said in a high-pitched voice that sounded almost childlike. She seemed in constant motion, jittery.

"That's not a problem," Kate said. "Actually, I heard that you're offering ballroom dance lessons—"

"Yes, yes!" Audrey clapped her hands together and led Kate to a stack of brochures on the piano. "My husband just designed these for me." She handed one to Kate.

The cover of the nicely done brochure pictured a couple in silhouette in a classic waltz pose, backs erect, heads pointing away from each other as if being pulled in an invisible tug-of-war.

"I'm amazed at how many people are signing up for classes," the woman said, looking at the pamphlet over Kate's shoulder. "I'm Audrey Harper. I know who you are—Kate Hanlon from Faith Briar. Actually, we met a few weeks ago after church."

"I remember." Kate smiled at her. The woman was difficult to forget.

Kate read the brochure and said, "Do you know which class Livvy and Danny Jenner signed up for?"

"Oh sure," Audrey said, pointing at the listing. "They're in the Tuesday-Thursday night class. We meet at seven."

"That starts this week?"

"Actually, it starts next week. I still have room for another couple if you're interested."

Just then the door opened and a man stepped in. He had white hair and was distinguished looking, with a trim waist and a healthy tan. Kate recognized him as Audrey's husband Hal, whom she'd also met at church a few weeks prior.

"Mrs. Hanlon." The man gave her a grin of recognition and held out a hand.

"Mrs. Hanlon is thinking about taking dance lessons," Audrey informed him.

His head bobbed once as he and Kate shook hands.

"Yes, I am," Kate said. "I somehow convinced Paul to agree, so I don't want to miss a good opportunity."

"Wonderful," Audrey said. "Once he gets the hang of it, he'll want to take you dancing all the time." She beamed at her husband. "Hal helps with the classes too. I can teach both the men's and ladies' parts, but it's so nice to be able to demonstrate the way a dance is supposed to look with both partners. You know?"

Kate looked at Hal, who seemed like the kind of man who was comfortable letting his wife shine. He made no further attempt to speak, merely smiled and nodded his head in agreement with Audrey.

Picking up an overstuffed leather bag from alongside the piano, she retrieved a green binder and shuffled through for the correct page.

"Here it is." She turned the book to face Kate. It was a sign-up page for the class. Kate noted several names she recognized, Danny and Livvy Jenner's among them.

Kate wrote down her information and paid for the classes, then said her farewells.

AGENT WIMPER CALLED Wednesday evening, asking if Paul knew of another way that they could get ahold of the Lovelace family on vacation. Paul had given them all the information he had, but they must not have been successful in contacting Millie and Boom.

For the next day, she wondered about it, but she couldn't—no, wouldn't—believe that someone from their church had anything to do with the scheme. Much less Millie Lovelace. She was a trusted friend. Sure, she had rough edges, but who didn't?

Yet the question of the money in the envelope and the handwritten note remained. *What had the Secret Service agents learned in their investigation?* she wondered. Millie was due home the next day, and Kate couldn't wait to talk to her.

KATE WAS ANXIOUS TO SPEAK with Millie about the envelope on Friday. Paul said that she would be back to her job at the SuperMart in Pine Ridge that afternoon, so after lunch, Kate hopped into her black Honda and drove the short distance to the neighboring town.

She made her way through the wide doors at the front of the store.

"Welcome to SuperMart," a friendly gray-haired man wearing a blue vest said.

Kate waved at him as she moved inside. She scanned the checkouts for Millie, unsure of where the church secretary would be working. She walked along the front of the building. No Millie. She moved into women's clothing, then children's. Still no sight of her.

Then Kate spied her behind the jewelry counter. She was just about to walk up to her to ask about the envelope when something in Millie's demeanor stopped her.

Millie glanced around as if she was afraid of being watched. Then she opened the cash drawer, pulled out a stack of bills, and replaced them with others she had laid beside her on the counter. She placed the bills from the register in a cloth sack that she quickly tied shut and tucked inside her blue SuperMart vest.

Kate watched in stunned silence. Surely she was mistaken. She hadn't seen what she thought she saw, had she?

Millie hadn't just replaced legitimate bills with counterfeits, had she? There had to be an explanation.

Chapter Seven

Kate tried to think of reasons why Millie would act as she had when she'd exchanged the bills. The way she'd looked around as if she didn't want anyone to see her . . . It didn't sit well with Kate. She hadn't had the nerve to talk to her, mostly because she didn't want to believe what she'd seen.

That night as they sat eating, Paul reached for Kate's hand across the supper table. "Something's bothering you," he said.

"I'm fine," she hedged.

Paul sat back in his chair. "I know you pretty well, Kate Hanlon. Something's up."

"I . . . saw something today . . ." She paused and looked Paul in the eye. Finally she sighed. "I went by the SuperMart to talk to Millie about that envelope."

"So what did she say?"

"Nothing. I didn't get a chance to actually talk to her. It was what she did . . ." Paul's brow puckered, and Kate went on. "She was acting *secretive*. I saw her exchanging money from a till."

"She could've been making change, getting a deposit ready," Paul offered, though his troubled look spoke of his concern.

"I thought of that, but it was the *way* she was acting—like she didn't want anyone to see her . . . Like she was—" She cut off her own words. What was she thinking? Millie was Paul's secretary. She was no counterfeiter.

THE SUPERMART STORE MANAGER, Randall Randolph, was an odd little man who never seemed to look anyone in the eyes. He fidgeted constantly, and if Kate were to hazard a guess, she would have said the man had attention deficit hyperactivity disorder; in her day, that had simply been called hyper.

She'd driven to the store on Sunday afternoon after lunch to investigate whether there was a good explanation for what she'd seen. There had to be some logical reason for Millie to have acted as she had. Millie hadn't made it to church that morning. So Kate couldn't talk to her then. She wasn't even sure what she'd say.

"Have you had any counterfeit bills show up?" Kate asked.

Kate and Randall were in the layaway section at the back of the store, he on one side of the counter and she on the other. The scent of fresh cardboard tickled her nose, giving her the urge to sneeze. Randall pushed his thick black glasses up on the bridge of his nose.

The man's eyes narrowed, and he pursed his lips as if considering his answer. "Why do you want to know?" He shrugged, then fidgeted with a pencil in his hand and wrote something on a stack of papers on the counter.

"There have been some counterfeits passed in Copper Mill. I wanted to determine how widespread it is."

"Uh-huh," he said. Kate could tell he knew there was more. "I don't know if you've ever worked retail, ma'am. But there are thieves everywhere. We catch them on the closed-circuit cameras. If anyone did anything suspicious, we would've seen it."

That gave Kate an idea. "Is there any way we could look at the footage from the past week?"

"Footage of what?" He cleared his throat.

"The jewelry counter?" Kate tried to make her voice sound natural.

"What exactly are you digging for?" Randall crossed his arms over his chest.

"I saw something when I was in here on Friday afternoon, and I just wanted to check it out . . ." Kate knew her explanation sounded weak, but she didn't want to mention Millie's name, especially if it was all a misunderstanding.

"Judy Dunn and Millie Lovelace worked the jewelry counter on Friday. I suppose it wouldn't hurt for you to talk to them." His eyes squinted to mere slits. "But we do have rules about privacy here." He sniffed.

"I appreciate that," Kate said, smiling at the man. "I really do. Is Judy here now?"

"Sorry, no. She'll be back Tuesday."

Kate sighed. She wasn't sure she could wait until then.

AFTER VISITING THE SUPERMART, Kate ran some errands in Pine Ridge. By the time she got home, it was getting late, so

Paul had put supper on for them. The scent of onions and green peppers frying filled the house with its mouthwatering aroma.

Kate moved into the bedroom and kicked off her shoes. She had just turned on the faucet in the adjacent bathroom to wash her hands when she heard the phone ring. Paul was still in the kitchen, and she assumed he would get it.

As she moved into the bedroom, took off her earrings, and set them in the small jewelry box on the dresser in her bedroom, her mind returned to her conversation with the store manager. When he spoke of thieves, did he have a particular person in mind? She wanted to ask the question outright—is it possible that Millie Lovelace passed counterfeit money at your store? But how could she without destroying Millie's reputation and career? If Millie was innocent, it would be inexcusable.

Then she heard Paul's voice. It sounded strained. Whom was he talking to? She made her way to the kitchen to see what was going on.

Paul's back was to the living room as he sat on a kitchen stool. "Amy, please try to calm down," he was saying. "Where is he now?"

Amy? Had something happened to Jake? Kate moved into the room and touched Paul on the shoulder. He glanced up at her and reached for her hand.

"Yes. That's okay. Really. Kate and I will be over in a few minutes. Do you have a lawyer?"

Kate puckered her brow. *What would they need a lawyer for?* Finally Paul hung up and turned to her.

"What's going on?" she said.

"Tim was arrested." He stood and reached for the car keys he'd laid on the counter, slipping them into his front pants pocket.

Kate stared at him, not comprehending what he'd just said. "Arrested? What for?"

"The Secret Service says he's the counterfeiter."

EVERY LIGHT WAS ON at the Lourdes' home. The sheriff's SUV and two dark sedans and several police cars were parked in front of the one-story house. Paul pulled up next to the curb and shut off the engine.

"I don't understand why they would think Tim did this," Kate said, shaking her head. "What could he possibly have to gain by putting fake bills into the offering when he could've simply slipped them in with real cash while working at the bank? It doesn't make sense to me." She climbed out of the car and shut the door.

"I'm sure they have some reason to suspect him. They don't arrest people without probable cause." By the gentle tone of Paul's voice, Kate knew he was merely stating the facts. He wasn't trying to be hard-hearted. "Let's just try to stay calm until we know what happened."

Paul was at her side as they made their way to the rambler's front door.

"How did Amy sound on the phone?" Kate whispered as they waited for someone to answer their knock.

"Terrified."

Kate's heart twisted.

Finally Agent Norris opened the door. "I'm sorry, but we're in the midst of an investigation . . . ," he began.

"I invited them," Kate heard Amy say from deeper in the room. "I needed moral support."

The Secret Service agent mumbled something to another person, then begrudgingly opened the door wider for Kate and Paul to enter. There were two agents in the house, as well as a plethora of police officers. Some took photographs, while others riffled through papers in the small den near the front that Amy said held Tim's home office and computer stuff.

The young wife looked devastated. Her pretty face was red from crying, and dark circles ringed her eyes. Her hair hung like a damp rag. She breathed a stuttering breath as if seeing Paul and Kate there might bring on another surge of tears. Kate closed the distance between them and enveloped her in a hug.

"Are you okay?" Kate murmured.

Amy didn't respond, though Kate felt the rigidity of her body and heard the quiet sigh she released when they pulled apart.

"They have this all wrong," Amy finally said, shaking her head. "Tim couldn't have done the things they're saying he did."

Kate didn't see Jake anywhere. She wondered if he was in his bedroom. "Where's Jake?"

"He's at the neighbor's. How do I tell him his dad is in jail when he comes home?" Her voice broke, and she paused to compose herself.

She swiped at her tears with her hand, and Kate opened

her handbag to get her a tissue. The bag was so full that she pulled several items out before finding the tissues at the bottom. She handed the packet to Amy, who accepted it gratefully.

"What did the officials tell you?" Paul asked, leading the way toward the small dining room, where they took seats around the table.

"Something about finding Tim's fingerprints on some of the bills and his having a motive and easy access to real bills. He's a bank official, so his prints were on file . . ." She shrugged and blew her nose. "It's ridiculous. He works at the bank—of course his prints could be on some of the bills."

"Did he say that to the Secret Service?" Kate said, though it occurred to her that as a bank official he should've turned in any counterfeit money or at least been able to spot it more easily than a non-banking person.

"Yeah . . . not that it made any difference." The cuckoo clock on the wall struck seven o'clock. The little bird dipped his head with each beat, then retreated behind the tiny wooden door.

"Where is Tim now?" Paul asked.

"He's in town, at the jail. They said he'll stay there until trial, and if he's found guilty, they'll move him to a federal facility."

"We can take you to go see him tomorrow if you'd like," Paul assured.

"Thank you," Amy said. "But I want to take Jake first thing, just the two of us."

Kate touched the young woman's shoulder to reassure her.

Amy rose to retrieve something from the letter organizer

on the kitchen counter adjacent to the dining room. "I want to give this back." It was the check Kate had dropped off from the previous Sunday's offering.

"No, you still need this," Kate said.

"Until Tim's name is cleared, I can't accept it. It doesn't sit right." She dropped it on the table in front of Kate, and Kate reluctantly tucked it into her handbag.

Just then, one agent and a police officer carried Tim's computer equipment out of the den in large boxes.

"What are you doing with that?" Amy was on her feet, moving between the men and the front door. Kate and Paul followed.

"That's Tim's stuff. You can't just take it." Her volume rose along with her anger.

"It's evidence, ma'am," Agent Norris said.

"It's no such thing!" Amy insisted. "Unless you found scans of dollar bills on the hard drive, I demand that you put it back. All of Jake's medical information is on that computer. We need it." She turned to Paul, desperation on her face.

But it was the agent who replied. "We have a search warrant, Reverend." He handed the document to Paul. "This is clearly within our jurisdiction." Then he nodded at Amy. "I'm sorry, ma'am."

Paul perused the warrant; Kate did as well, noting the right to seize evidence.

Then Paul took Amy by the elbow and said gently to her, "We'll let them have a look, okay? They'll get it all back to you. Right?" He glanced at the agent, who shrugged.

"Not if we find what we think we'll find," the agent said.

Kate wished the man had more tact.

"This isn't right!" Amy said, twisting away from Paul's grasp. "My calendar is on there—all of Jake's treatments, new discoveries for treating CF . . ." Her voice cracked with emotion.

"We'll help you find a lawyer," Kate offered as she placed a comforting hand on Amy's back. "First thing in the morning."

Chapter Eight

The next day was cloudy and gloomy. Rain was in the forecast, though it hadn't yet begun to fall. Close to noon, Kate and Paul drove to the jail that was housed in the Copper Mill Town Hall.

Tim Lourdes. Kate couldn't get over the shock of the news, though she realized she didn't know the man. What *did* she know of him? Other than that he had an ill child, had just moved to town and worked at the bank, she knew nothing.

She and Paul had stayed with Amy until after ten the previous night. The neighbor brought Jake home long after the police and Secret Service left, which Kate was glad for, though she didn't miss the accusing looks the woman sent in Amy's direction. Thankfully, Amy seemed too distraught to notice.

Jake had cried and cried when Amy told him the news. His pale face was blotchy from tears, and his body shook with rattling bouts as his cystic fibrosis made itself known. An image of Amy holding him burned into Kate's mind.

When Paul and Kate had finally left, Amy said she'd be all right, though Kate doubted the young wife would get much sleep. Kate didn't either. Confusion warred within her. How had Tim Lourdes become the suspect when evidence seemed to point to Millie? Were either of them capable of the crime? She'd lain awake all night, thinking about it.

Paul had made a call to a lawyer in Pine Ridge shortly after eight o'clock the next morning, though they had been told that a court-appointed attorney would be available to Tim if he needed one. The man, whom Paul said sounded like he was in his late eighties, promised to call Amy later in the day to discuss the case as well as his costs.

Kate's thoughts were interrupted when they parked near the Copper Mill Town Hall. The town hall was a no-nonsense two-story brick building with off-white trim. Maple trees lined the walkway leading to the concrete stairs and the double glass-door entrance. A breeze ruffled the leaves overhead.

When they entered the deputy's office, Skip Spencer was at his desk, his head bent over paperwork. Kate and Paul moved alongside him.

"Mrs. Hanlon . . . Pastor." Skip's face lit in a slow smile when he lifted his face. "What can I do you for?"

"We're here to see Tim Lourdes," Paul said.

"His wife and son were just here," he informed them.

Kate nodded at the deputy. "How does he seem?" she asked.

"Hard to say." Skip shrugged.

"Do you think he's guilty?" she asked.

"Trust me, the Secret Service wouldn't have nailed him if they didn't have solid proof." He leaned forward and lowered his voice even though they were the only ones in the small room. "Think about it. He just moved to Copper Mill. No one knows him. He doesn't even have family here. He gets a job at the bank; it's the perfect cover for a counterfeiter. He's smart. They say he's real good with computers, which a counterfeiter would have to be in this day and age. His family is struggling with finances . . ." His words trailed away.

"Can we see him?" Paul asked.

"Oh yeah, of course." Skip got to his feet and retrieved the keys from their hook behind the door.

He led Kate and Paul across the hall to the first of the two cells the town hall housed. The keys on the large ring jangled when he raised them to unlock the cell.

Tim lifted his face. He looked as devastated as his wife had the night before. He gave a halfhearted smile when Kate and Paul joined him in the cell, the door clanging shut behind them.

Skip excused himself, his boots echoing as he walked away. Paul sat next to Tim on the lone cot in the small room. Kate took the single hard plastic chair across from them.

"How was your visit with Amy and Jake this morning?" Kate asked.

The agony in his eyes was difficult to deny. "Hard," he said. "This isn't real. It's too bizarre . . . I worry about them."

"Amy's shaken," Kate said. "As anyone would be, but she's a strong woman. She'll be okay. Jake's a trooper."

Tim exhaled a shuddering breath, though he nodded his agreement.

"Did you have any idea that you were a suspect?" Paul asked.

"None. The Secret Service asked me some questions at work, but they questioned a lot of people. I don't get it. I didn't do this." He looked at Kate, and she studied his face. His eyes were wide, almost pleading. "They said my prints were on the counterfeits."

"The ones from the offering?" Kate asked.

Tim shook his head. "No. They said there were too many prints overlapping to tell on those. It was the ones they found at the bank."

"Do you ever fill in for the tellers?" Kate asked.

"All the time. We all do. When someone has to take a break, one of the loan officers will take over till they get back. I don't understand what's so unusual about that. If that's all they're basing this on . . ." He shook his head.

As Kate watched him, saw the waves of devastation crash across his face, she wondered if it was possible for someone to act so convincingly innocent and yet be guilty.

Of course, she knew it was entirely possible.

SHERIFF ROBERTS was in the deputy's office when Kate and Paul returned with Skip after their talk with Tim. Agent Norris was there too. Skip placed the cell's keys back on their hook and repositioned himself in his chair.

"We're sending the computer to our specialist," Norris was saying to the sheriff. "Lourdes has passwords on everything."

"Excuse me," Kate said to the agent. The men turned to face her. "Can I ask what it was that made you realize it was Tim?"

The man didn't hesitate. "The fingerprints." He had a smug expression on his face, a stark contrast to the agony Kate had just witnessed in Tim. "As a loan officer, he shouldn't have been handling the cash like a teller, yet there were several bills with his prints. I'm sure that once we hack into his computer, we'll find enough evidence to put him away for a very long time."

"The counterfeits felt like real money," she observed. "Did your experts have an explanation for that?"

The agent furrowed his brow as if he didn't like her questions.

"I didn't mean to pry," Kate quickly said. "I'm just curious." She felt her face flame.

"The thing now is," the agent offered, "even though we have Mr. Lourdes in custody, any bills that surface could simply be ones that he put into circulation earlier—there's no way to know. And if he had an accomplice, perhaps his wife . . ."

Amy? Kate couldn't imagine the devoted wife and mother involved in anything like counterfeiting.

THE CAR RIDE HOME WAS QUIET. Kate gazed out the window as Paul turned up Smoky Mountain Road. Heat shimmered on the road's surface, creating a miragelike wave ahead.

Finally Kate broke the silence. "Do you think he did it?"

Paul shook his head. "Hard to say. He comes off as a very sincere person, and I can't imagine Amy being an accomplice."

"It seems like they have enough on their plate just dealing with Jake's cystic fibrosis. I keep seeing the image of that little boy swinging his feet in church while his father talked about his needs. It doesn't seem to jibe."

Paul nodded in agreement.

Kate went on, processing for herself as much as with

Paul. "And yet people who are desperate do all kinds of strange things."

"They do have the fingerprints . . . ," Paul added.

Kate nodded. "Not on the offering bills, yet Agent Norris still says Tim's guilty. But why would Tim place cash in the offering that was meant to go to his own family? That doesn't add up to me."

"Maybe he thought the bills wouldn't be detected in the deposit, that it'd be easier to pass off."

"That's possible, I guess." Kate let out a heavy breath. If Tim had committed this crime, what would become of his son? That was the most troubling thought of all. And if Amy were involved?

Kate sighed and looked in her handbag for her cell phone. She wanted to call around about what she'd learned in her own sleuthing. Had she been on the wrong trail all along? She moved her hand around, scraping the bottom of her purse. As she riffled around, she realized something was missing. Her camera had been in here.

"Didn't I have my camera in here last Sunday?" she asked Paul.

"I remember you showing a picture of the Lourdes family to Livvy and Danny at the diner on Monday," Paul confirmed.

Kate pushed the contents of her handbag around one more time. She found the phone, but no camera. "Maybe I took it out when I got Amy those tissues last night." Kate tried not to panic.

"Maybe." As he said it, Kate's cell phone rang in her hand. She glanced at the display. *Amy Lourdes*.

Taking a deep breath, she accepted the call. "Hi, Amy," she said.

"Hey, Kate." The young mother sounded tired. "I'm sorry to bug you, but could you come by the house?"

Kate mouthed the request to Paul, who nodded and turned the car back toward town.

"Of course. We're on our way."

WHEN THEY ARRIVED, Jake wasn't home. Amy explained that he'd gone to play at the neighbor's again.

Kate patted her shoulder and followed her to the small living room, with Paul close behind.

Once they were seated, Amy said, "That lawyer in Pine Ridge called." She shook her head. "There's no way we can afford him. We'll have to hope the court-appointed attorney is competent."

Her eyes filled with worry, and she took a sip of water from a glass on the low coffee table between them. "I was supposed to take Jake in to the children's hospital today. The doctor wanted to see how his new asthma medicine is working." A tear slid down her cheek.

"Do you want me to take him?" Kate offered.

Amy shook her head. "I canceled the appointment." She took a deep breath. "Right now I have to prove Tim's innocence—somehow. He *is* innocent."

She looked deep into Kate's eyes as if hoping to find agreement there. But Kate wasn't sure of anything at this point, though she couldn't bring herself to say that to the hurting woman.

Just then, Jake came bounding in the front door in a flurry of noise and door slamming. His face was red, and he was breathing heavily when he came around the corner.

"Hey, buddy," his mother said. Trouble brewed in his eyes. "What's wrong?"

Jake's thin frame moved with each breath. Then he said, in that voice that sounded as if he had a cold, "Is Dad a thief?"

"Where did you hear that?" Amy moved to him.

"Is it true?" The six-year-old stared at his mother, his pale face filled with hope that the words were wrong. He coughed again, an unsettling sound.

"No, baby." Amy bent to wipe his tear-stained face. "It is definitely not true. You and I know Daddy better than anyone in the world, and we know that he isn't that kind of person." She challenged him to be strong with her eyes. "You know that, right?"

Jake finally nodded.

"People can be mean, but that doesn't make what they say true. Okay?"

Gradually the boy seemed to calm himself. He took a deep breath. Then he started coughing, and Amy patted his back. When the bout had passed, he shifted awkwardly, and Amy said, "Go get your chest clapper."

Jake glanced at Kate and Paul.

"Go," his mother insisted. Then she excused herself to help him set up the device. They disappeared into the bedroom at the back of the long hall, only the sounds of Jake coughing, gagging and choking along with Amy's words of comfort reaching Paul and Kate in the living room. They said nothing, though Kate thought her heart would break.

After a good fifteen minutes, Amy returned to take her seat alongside Kate and said, "I'm sorry about all that." She looked fragile, ready to come apart.

Tears glistened on her lower lashes. "We have to prove that Tim is innocent," she said. "I can't do this alone. Please help me. Help us." Her gaze shifted between Kate and Paul.

Conviction grew in Kate's heart. This wasn't just about proving that the guilty party wasn't from Faith Briar, though a large part of her hoped for that. She knew now that for Jake's sake, she needed to help the Lourdeses. She needed to find the truth. She needed to find the people responsible.

Chapter Nine

Kate had asked Amy about the missing camera during their visit, but it was nowhere to be found. Amy said she recalled seeing her take it from her handbag on Sunday night when Kate had gotten the tissues, but she hadn't seen it since. They'd searched the house, even rooms that Kate hadn't been in during her prior visit, thinking Jake might've taken it somewhere. But it was gone. Kate tried to remember where she'd put it. She'd called the Country Diner to see if she'd forgotten it there, but no one had seen it.

But another question had yet to be answered—the matter of Millie's strange behavior at the SuperMart. She needed to settle that matter once and for all so she could move on. So Tuesday, she climbed into her car yet again to head to the megastore.

Judy Dunn, the clerk who worked the jewelry counter alongside Millie Lovelace, stared through thick Coke-bottle glasses at Kate. Her black hair stood off her head as if she were being electrocuted. Despite her dated attire, she seemed to be quite young—in her twenties, Kate guessed.

"Did you say you were with the FBI?" she said in a nasally voice, her attention somewhere over Kate's shoulder.

"I'm just helping a friend," Kate said with a smile. "Do you always work the jewelry counter?"

Judy shook her head. "Depends on what Randall wants me to do."

"Do you know if any counterfeit bills showed up at the jewelry counter last week?"

The young woman's face blanched. "Counterfeits? Randall didn't say anything about counterfeits. Does he think I accepted them?"

"No," Kate assured her. "He said you might be able to talk to me about any . . . possibly unusual activities at the jewelry counter from last Friday?" She pointed to the black dome on the ceiling that concealed the cameras positioned throughout the store.

"Oh." Judy's mouth dropped open. She turned a puzzled look to Kate. "Why do you want to know about that?"

"It's hard to explain," Kate said, careful not to start any rumors about Millie. "I thought I witnessed something when I was here on Friday . . ." Kate let the words trail away.

The salesclerk studied Kate for a long moment, then picked up the phone. She talked in hushed tones, Kate assumed to Randall, given the furtive glances she sent to Kate.

"Can I show her the footage?" Judy was saying. "Oh . . . okay. How many times has she been here?" There was a long pause while she listened. "I have no idea." Then she hung up, leveled a look at Kate, and said, "Randall said you can look for yourself."

What had brought about the man's change of heart? Kate wondered, though she wasn't about to argue.

Judy guided Kate across the sales floor and through a door marked Employees Only. She led Kate through a maze of boxes in the back of the store and up to the security section. A guard sat at a desk staring at monitor after monitor, and lifted his head when Judy and Kate came in.

"Kent," Judy said, "can you find the footage of last Friday at the jewelry counter?"

The man narrowed his eyes at Kate, and Judy assured, "She's okay."

The heavyset man slowly got up and shuffled to the other side of the room. He found the tape with the footage of Millie stuffing the cash into her vest. There in front of them was the moment in question: Millie glancing around. Placing the sack of money alongside the till, then switching the bills.

Judy sat back in shock. And Kent said, "What in the world is she doing?" He scratched the top of his head.

"You think there's something to it? What should we do?" Judy finally said when the security guard turned off the monitor.

THE SECRET SERVICE AGENT seemed almost irritated as he reviewed the footage in the crowded back room of the SuperMart. He leaned in for a closer look, then he blew out a heavy breath as he raked a hand through his blond hair.

"What do you think she's doing?" Kate asked.

The agent's blue eyes landed on her. There was a sense of condescension in his expression that Kate brushed aside.

"Mrs. Hanlon," he began. "I appreciate that you brought

this information to my attention, but the truth is, none of the counterfeit bills have surfaced at SuperMart or in Pine Ridge." He shook his head at her. "And we have arrested our criminal. The only thing we don't have is the accomplice. Are you accusing Mrs. Lovelace of being the accomplice?"

"No . . . I don't know," Kate said sheepishly. She had to admit she was relieved that Agent Norris didn't suspect Millie was a part of the crime, but the agent had yet to explain her strange behavior.

His expression softened. "Listen, I appreciate that you care about Mr. Lourdes and want to see him back with his family. But maybe you should ask yourself just how well you know him."

KATE GLANCED OUT the large dance studio windows, distracted by her conversation with Agent Norris earlier that day. He had asked her to move on, but didn't he have any doubts at all? Hadn't he spoken to Tim and seen his sincerity? Was sincerity enough to prove innocence?

Kate turned back to the room of dance students, who were chatting among themselves. There were a few couples Kate didn't recognize. The two Cline sisters, who worked as tellers at the Mid-Cumberland Bank, were there, though Kate didn't see any dance partners for them. The women stood to the side, their blue hair forming a peak as they whispered to each other. Renee Lambert was there with Sam Gorman. Kate wondered how the seventy-one-year-old woman had convinced the younger man to agree to take dance lessons. Paul gave him a wave, and his face broke into a grin. Livvy and Danny Jenner were there also, standing near the back of the room. Kate waved and led Paul to them.

Kate didn't see Audrey or Hal anywhere, though there was soft music wafting from a CD player atop the piano.

Livvy was glancing around the room. "It's quite a turnout, isn't it? This is going to be fun."

"Have you taken any kind of lessons before?" Kate asked Danny.

"Just square dancing in grade school."

"Swing your partner, do-si-do," Kate said and Livvy giggled.

Finally Audrey came into the room, wearing a flowing aqua blue caftan that reached almost to the floor. Her white, high-heeled sandals peeked from beneath. Her jewelry was big and gaudy and made a tinkling sound as she clapped her hands in three quick raps.

"Gather up, now," she said in her high-pitched voice, a smile on her paper-white face.

Everyone quieted down. Hal had come in behind her and stood to the side with his hands clasped in front of him. When Kate met his eye, he nodded briefly.

Paul had come to stand behind Kate as Audrey began introductions.

"Welcome to beginning waltz." She turned to take in the whole class, then pointed out her husband as coteacher for the class.

"Now y'all are gonna have to help me with your names. I'm not much for such details unless it has to do with dancing." She laughed in her nervous way, and a few of the students chuckled along. "We'll take it slow, so you don't need to fret.

Hal and I will show you everything first. Then we'll come around to help couples."

The class formed a circle around the room, leaving the center open for Audrey and Hal. Audrey slipped a CD into the changer, then took her position in her husband's arms.

Audrey and Hal stood like the silhouette Kate had seen on the brochure, tall and elegant as the music began.

They mesmerized their spectators like a couple deeply in love. The expression in Hal's eyes mirrored the look Kate often saw in her own husband's face—years of devotion. One step moved into the next and the next in a fluidity of motion and symmetry. They seemed lost in each other, and Kate found herself blushing at the sense that she was intruding on a private moment. Several minutes later, the music ceased.

They moved directly into lessons, teaching the basic box step, then gathering everyone up in pairs like animals on the ark.

"Tell me if I step on your toes," Paul said as he took hold of Kate's waist.

"I'll be sure to yelp." Kate smirked.

Audrey was talking again. "You two, where are your partners?" She was speaking to Georgia and Evelyn Cline.

The identical twins, who stood facing each other, burned with embarrassment. Kate had a hard time telling the two apart, especially when they weren't together.

"We couldn't find partners, so we're dancing together," Georgia said. "That's not a problem, is it?"

It sounded to Kate's ears almost like a threat. *I dare you to kick paying customers out of your class.*

"It's not a problem at all, honey." The endearment was spoken gently, carrying a measure of grace for their transgression. "I'll share Hal with you so you both can get the feel of following. We don't want to have you domineering any potential dance partners down the road, do we?" Her head bobbed slightly with the joke.

Georgia cleared her throat, while Evelyn nodded in agreement.

Kate grinned up at Paul.

"Let's see if we can teach this old dog a new trick," he said.

Kate smiled at him. It felt good to try something new with an old dog.

Chapter Ten

Images of Tim Lourdes in jail and Millie Lovelace stuffing money into her SuperMart vest haunted Kate all through the night.

So Wednesday morning, after she'd spent some time in the Word and cleaned up from breakfast, she headed to the church to see Millie. Paul had gone to do some visitation at the hospital in Pine Ridge, and Kate was glad to have a private moment with the church secretary.

Kate felt sure she read more into what she'd seen than was there. Yet how could she broach the subject?

Um, Millie, I was spying on you at SuperMart on Friday, and I talked to the Secret Service about you . . . No, that wasn't right. *Did you happen to steal a sack of money from the jewelry counter?* No, that didn't work either. She'd simply ask about the mysterious envelope as she'd meant to do before. Hopefully, the conversation would transition naturally from there.

Kate drummed her fingers on the steering wheel as she drove the short distance to the church. Millie's red Nissan was parked in the lot. Kate pulled her black Honda alongside it and made her way inside.

The gruff little woman lifted her head when Kate came around the corner. “What are you doing here, Kate?” Millie said curtly.

Kate cleared her throat, buying herself a few moments.

“How was your vacation?” she began.

“It was good.” That was all Millie offered. She watched Kate for a moment.

She should’ve known Millie wouldn’t appreciate small talk. “Did you see an envelope for the Lourdes’ offering before you left on vacation?” Kate decided to dig right in.

“Of course.” Millie turned back to the computer. “I put it in my desk tray for you. It was part of the money for the special offering. There was a note on it.”

“So you wrote that note?”

Millie nodded.

“Did you know that some of the money was counterfeit?”

A look came over the woman’s face slowly, and Kate wasn’t sure how to read it. It was as if someone had told a joke she hadn’t quite gotten at first, but then the meaning dawned piece by piece. “They think the counterfeit money came from that envelope?”

Kate took the chair across from her. “They aren’t sure,” she said. “It could’ve come from passing the plate that Sunday or from the envelope. I was hoping you could shed some light on where the envelope came from.”

“A woman brought it by.” She shrugged her shoulders. “I didn’t examine it closely.”

“But do you know who she was?”

"She said she'd heard about the offering and wanted to help." She clicked a few keys on her keyboard.

"What did she look like?"

"She was tall and had dark hair, brown, I think. She seemed nice."

"Would you recognize her if you saw her again?"

Millie shook her head. "I didn't really pay close attention. She dropped it off and left."

"Did you write both notes?"

"Both?"

"There was a note that said 'Don't forget twenties and fifties.'"

Millie waved her hand as if she were waving away a gnat. "That was a note to myself, so I'd remember to get cash for vacation. I have no idea how it came to be on the envelope. I heard somewhere that they didn't take credit cards at Disney. By the way, that's not true."

The image of Millie stuffing the bag of money into her vest flashed into Kate's mind.

"You've been back at the SuperMart for a few days?" Kate probed.

Millie gave her a puzzled look. "Uh-huh."

"Has there been anything"—she searched for the right word—"*unusual* there?" She hoped it would be enough for Millie to pick up on.

Millie gave her a blank look. "Unusual?" Millie paused for a moment as if in thought. "There was a robbery at the SuperMart the day before I got back, if that's what you're talking about."

"A robbery?" Why hadn't anyone else mentioned it?

"It really rattled me," she added with a shrug and a humorless chuckle.

"That would scare me too," Kate said. "Did they catch the perpetrator?"

"Yeah, some kid from out of town. They arrested him Saturday."

Relief filled Kate. A robbery. That could explain why Millie had acted so nervous with the cash. Maybe she was simply paranoid that the robber was still around.

When Kate left for home, she called Randall Randolph, who confirmed that there had been a robbery while Millie had been away. As it turned out, there hadn't been any money missing from the jewelry counter the Friday in question, nor had any counterfeit bills made an appearance.

Chapter Eleven

Renee Lambert called Kate on Thursday afternoon with news that more counterfeits had surfaced—some at the Mercantile and others at Emma's Ice Cream Shop. She told Kate that the authorities suspected the bills were passed the previous evening.

Passing the counterfeits with the town on full alert was pretty nervy, Kate thought.

Getting out a bread pan, she began what she often did when she had much to consider: she baked. This time it was her mother's special banana-bread recipe—no nuts, but so rich and moist it never lasted more than an hour or two after baking. At least not when Paul was in the house.

As she mashed the overripe bananas, several thoughts came. Who was the dark-haired woman who'd brought the envelope to Millie? Had the counterfeit bills come from that envelope or from the offering plates? What did the locations where the bills were passed have in common? Then it came to her—besides the bills passed at the church, both the Mercantile and Emma's employed young clerks.

It was much easier to get a counterfeit bill past inexperienced eyes.

Except the bank—everyone there was more than experienced, especially when it came to spotting phony money.

AN HOUR LATER, as the delicious-smelling bread came out of the oven, Kate decided to pay a visit to the library and then to Amy afterward. She wrapped the still-warm bread in foil to take to the Lourdes', then hopped into her black Honda to head to town.

Livvy stood at her post behind the horseshoe-shaped counter near the library entrance. "What's up?" she said.

"Hey, Liv. I'm just here to enjoy some of your high-speed Internet." With only a dial-up connection at home, Kate often found it faster to use the library's computers.

"Of course," Livvy said. "How are the Lourdeses doing?" she asked. "I keep thinking about that poor little boy . . ."

"I know. You should've seen the look on Tim's face when Paul and I went to see him. He's devastated and frantic to get back to his family. He's so worried about Jake."

"I'm glad you're looking into who did this," Livvy said with a knowing gleam in her eyes. Kate had felt a connection with Livvy practically from the first time they'd met, as if she were a long-lost sister.

Kate nodded and made her way to the upstairs computer bank. She began her search, punching into Google the words *counterfeiting* and *how to*.

She clicked on a site and learned that rag paper was the cotton-linen mix upon which genuine money was printed. It had a high fabric content, which explained why you could wash money in the laundry and not have it disintegrate as a sheet of printer paper would.

Kate paused in thought. The bills in the offering had that *feel* of true money. How had the counterfeiter duplicated it? She typed "papermaking" and read about what it took to create the thin fabric-paper. It wasn't an easy feat, that was for sure. It required special rollers to press it thin, not to mention the watermark that bills had as part of their security feature.

Getting out the magnifying glass she'd put in her handbag, Kate pulled out several real dollar bills, examining them closely and noting the fine lines and various inks used.

Every site Kate looked at said that to spot fake money, you had to know what real money looked like. Real money was intricate in its design. It had multiple colors of inks, as well as magnetic inks and strips that allowed vending machines to read its value and thus dispense correct change. The level of detail in the bills was astounding.

As Kate read, she thought of how that principle was true of people too. The contrast between someone whose life was genuine and connected to God in a meaningful way was a stark contrast to those who only acted like people of faith when it suited their fancy. And while many looked like the real deal, it was at the heart level—that watermark placed by God—where the truth of their identity lay. It was what pushed her toward her belief that Tim Lourdes was innocent.

Then Kate clicked onto another page that recounted cases of counterfeiters caught in the act. As the printing industry became more high-tech, she discovered, it took more and more expertise to pull off the feat of creating fakes. Whoever had made the bills knew what they were doing. Enough of the bills had been passed in town to attest to the quality of the counterfeit bills.

Kate clicked on a short video clip on the Secret Service's Web site and watched. When it finished, she noted an elderly woman peering over her shoulder at the screen.

"It's a crying shame, isn't it?" the woman said. "I had some of that funny money show up at my garage sale last week!"

Kate spun around in her chair. "Do you know who it came from?"

The woman shook her head. "It was a busy day—hard to know who did what. But I guarantee it was that new banker in town." The woman crossed her arms over her chest.

"Oh? Did you tell the Secret Service that?"

"Well, of course I did. I'm not un-American."

"What makes you certain it was him?"

"It just makes sense, doesn't it? It's always easier for an *insider* to get away with things like that."

It seemed the town had already tried and convicted Tim Lourdes. Yet doubt niggled at Kate. Yes, there were clues that pointed to him, but her instinct was that his character pointed in the opposite direction.

ONCE SHE'D FINISHED at the library, Kate made her way to the Lourdes' home. Amy was in the midst of preparing supper when Kate got there.

"Come in," Amy said, ushering her inside the neat home.

"You look busy," Kate began. She handed Amy the banana bread as she came inside.

"What's this?"

"My mother's banana-bread recipe. I thought you'd enjoy it."

Amy looked better, though the dark circles under her eyes remained. Her hair was tied neatly into a ponytail. She even wore a touch of makeup.

"It smells delicious. Thank you."

Amy led Kate to the kitchen just off the dining area in the small house. Jake was immersed in an episode of *Bugs Bunny* in the living room on the other side of the dining area. Kate recalled her own children, now grown, watching the same episode, a musical spoof of the *Barber of Seville*, and laughing as heartily as Jake did now, though his laughter was interspersed with that deep cough.

"We just got back from seeing Tim," Amy said, her voice low. "The public defender was there too; he didn't seem too optimistic about the case." She shook her head and let out a long breath. "They found *files* . . ."

"What kind of files?"

"I can't imagine. That computer had our basic family stuff on it—nothing illegal." Her face filled with horror.

"Amy," Kate reached for her hand and waited for her to compose herself. The young woman inhaled deeply. "Did anyone have access to Tim's computer?"

Amy shook her head. "Other than me? No one." She paused for a long moment. "I can't imagine what they found. Someone is doing this, Kate. Someone is setting Tim up."

Kate said a quick prayer for the distraught woman.

"Tell me about you and Tim," Kate said. "Has he ever been in any kind of trouble before?"

"No." Amy shook her head. "Except . . . well, we had some financial issues a while back." She took a deep breath. "Our last house was foreclosed on. With all of Jake's medical bills . . . it's been hard to make ends meet. The lawyer said that would hurt our case if the jury finds that out. "

It wasn't a secret that they'd had financial struggles, though the revelation of their foreclosure surely wouldn't help.

"So the lawyer thinks the jury will see a motive?"

Amy nodded.

So there were fingerprints, computer evidence—whatever that was—and motive. She wondered if she were on the jury whether she'd be able to overlook that evidence. So many questions remained.

"I guess we're at God's mercy." Amy smiled. "And I can think of worse places to be."

The young woman's faith through her adversity touched Kate. Many would turn their backs, or even blame God at a time like this, but Amy chose to trust him. Kate sent up a quick prayer for her.

Then she glanced at Amy as she returned to chopping tomatoes for tacos. She slipped the cut pieces into a multi-colored glass bowl before moving on to the onions and black olives.

"Amy, do you know what kind of printer and scanner Tim had?"

"The Secret Service confiscated them, but I have the paperwork on them."

"Could I take a look?"

"Of course." Amy wiped her hands on a towel and disappeared into the den at the front of the house while Kate waited at the kitchen counter. Jake began to cough so furiously that Kate came around the corner to check on him. His thin body convulsed with each burst. She patted his back, hoping to help him through the bout. When it finally ended, Jake stared up at her.

"You can pound on my back when that happens," he informed her. She patted a bit harder. "No, really *hit* me." But Kate was hesitant.

"He's right," Amy said, coming alongside them with the promised file folders in hand. She gave them to Kate, then leaned Jake forward and pounded what seemed to Kate to be too hard between his shoulder blades, starting low on his back and working upward with repeated, even blows.

"It's part of his physical therapy, to loosen that thick mucus that builds up in his lungs," she explained.

The boy coughed again, and Amy handed him several tissues. When it seemed he was finally freed from the hacking torture, he looked back at the TV show as if nothing had happened at all.

"Of course, with the asthma he has the nebulizer to help him breathe easier too," Amy said. "Something is bound to help, right? At least that's the hope."

She went back to supper preparations, and Kate laid the folders on the counter and paged through the contents of the first one. The documents were basic users' manuals, nothing exciting about them.

"Can I borrow these?" Kate asked.

Amy nodded as she kept chopping black olives on the cutting board between them. "I don't exactly need them right now."

"And . . . ," Kate paused, causing Amy to glance up, "would it be okay if I took a look at your basement and maybe your garage?"

"Look to your heart's content," she said with a smile.

Amy showed Kate the stairs to the basement and left her to explore on her own. The basement was mostly storage, with a laundry room and small weight room set up with a bench and dumbbells. But there was nothing of particular interest to Kate. No counterfeiting lab designed to reproduce bills, no papermaking equipment, not even a ream of paper for printing.

She searched the garage, which was mostly empty save for a lawn mower and a few gardening tools, then came back to the kitchen. Amy was setting the table.

Kate said, "Did the Secret Service confiscate anything else, other than Tim's computer, printer and scanner?"

"No," Amy said. "Except they took our bank statements and some other paperwork."

"But there wasn't anything else—no hardware, nothing from the basement or garage?"

"No, nothing else," Amy said.

Kate tapped a finger to her chin as she considered the implications of that information. It meant that if Tim was guilty, the bills had been made exclusively with the computer equipment. Unless he'd created them at another location. Either way, was it possible to create realistic money with those tools? Kate wasn't sure.

Chapter Twelve

Kate and Paul were the first to arrive for their second ballroom dance lesson on Thursday evening. Hal and Audrey greeted them at the door.

"So," Kate said, "how's life in Copper Mill so far? Are you beginning to feel at home?"

"Oh yes. Everyone has been so nice," Audrey said. "And I finally feel as if the house is getting settled. I don't ever want to see another box!"

"Where did you move from?" Paul asked.

"New York," Hal answered. "Lived there for a long time."

Audrey added, "So now he's retired, and we're living our dream."

"Do you have family in the area?" Kate asked.

Hal shook his head, while Audrey said, "We don't have much family to speak of, actually. Never had children, so it's just us."

"So why Copper Mill?" Paul asked.

Audrey shrugged, glancing at her husband. "We'd come through on vacation several years back and thought it was a nice place."

"That's courageous," Kate said. "To pick a spot on the map and move there without even a job waiting for you there."

"I'm pretty outgoing," Audrey said, "and we've moved around a bit in our married life, so it's not anything new for us. Now Hal"—she looked at her husband—"he's the shy one. But we're working on that." She winked.

Kate liked this couple. Audrey was a natural with people, and while Hal tended to be quieter than his vivacious wife, he seemed like a genteel man, offering smiles and agreeable nods.

Audrey and Hal went to greet the rest of the students as they came in—the Jenners, Renee Lambert, and Sam Gorman.

The Cline sisters came in last. Georgia, the older of the identical twins by five minutes, seemed perturbed about something. "I can't believe you could think that," she was saying to Evelyn. "He's been acting odd, if you ask me. Always leaving work to run off to this or that appointment. I'd think the mother could do that and not make Tim have to skip his responsibilities for it."

Defensiveness rose up in Kate when she realized they were talking about Tim Lourdes, though she decided it was best not to say anything.

Evelyn retorted, "Maybe Tim is simply a good father who wants to be around for his kid's doctor's appointments. That doesn't make him a criminal, does it?" Her head turned toward Kate as she spoke.

"Are you talking about that Lourdes family?" Audrey said instead.

Evelyn nodded. "We work with him at the bank; he's a nice kid."

"He's a crook," Georgia said under her breath. "His fingerprints had no business being on those bills—"

"I've been hearing about their situation around town," Audrey interrupted. "It must be impossibly difficult for his family, don't you agree? With that sick child and all."

Sam moved next to Paul and Kate to say hello.

"By the way, you never told me how Renee talked you into this," Kate heard Paul whisper to his friend.

"Beats me." Sam's eyes crinkled in a wizened way, and his skin had a tanned, ruddy appearance. "One minute we're talking about not much special—the price of gasoline and whatnot—the next she has me wrangled into taking dance lessons with her. It's like dancing with my Aunt Inez. She pinches my arm if I get it wrong!" He rubbed his upper arm where the offenses had occurred.

The three of them laughed.

Audrey moved to her spot to begin the class. "Everyone." She gave three short claps in front of her face, and the class quieted down. "Let's form two lines."

The men ambled to one side of the room while the women formed a line along the other. They went through the steps and were soon paired up again, the Cline sisters dancing with each other. They kept arguing as they danced, and Kate wondered why they continued to dance together when it was clear they weren't getting along.

Finally Hal came over. He smiled at each of the sisters in turn, then said, "Can I show you?" He lifted his hands into waltz position and spun Evelyn around the room. The younger of the two was a natural on the floor. Her body lifted and lowered along with Hal's as they moved in a spiraling pattern. Kate and Paul had stopped to watch them, unaware at first that Georgia was glowering at their admiration.

"She's good," Kate offered, but judging from the expression on Georgia's face, the comment didn't go over well.

"We're looking for *male* partners," Georgia informed. "Some of us aren't blessed with husbands who'll do whatever we wish."

Paul was smirking. Sam Gorman must've overheard too, because he shot a look at them that clearly said, *I am not Renee Lambert's puppet!* Renee danced blissfully on, though Kate did note that she gave Sam a pinch on the arm.

Hal brought Evelyn back to her sister so he could take a spin with the elder sister. Georgia didn't have the same ease Evelyn had shown, though she was still a fair dancer.

Paul tapped Kate on the shoulder and said, "Shall we?"

Kate laughed. She hadn't realized what a voyeur she'd become.

When Hal brought Georgia to her sister, he said, "You're both very natural dancers."

"You should think about entering the beginners' competition at the Pine Ridge Country Club next month," Audrey put in, coming behind her husband. "If the two of you can find partners, you'd do real well."

She looked to Paul and Kate and added, "You could enter it too, Mr. and Mrs. Hanlon."

"A competition?" Georgia perked up, a smug expression stealing across her face.

"There's even prize money for the winner," Audrey said.

Renee Lambert and Sam Gorman danced closer, and Renee said, "Is that open to just anyone?"

Sam shook his head vigorously.

"I am not making a fool of myself at any dance competition," Sam said. "Sorry, Renee, but you can look for a new partner too."

Renee's mouth opened and closed like a landed trout.

"Do you really think we'd do well?" Georgia went on.

"Absolutely," Audrey said with a smile. "But you can't dance with your sister! The judges would frown on that. Tell you what," she went on, "Hal and I have a competition coming up in Pine Ridge. Come and see what it's like. If any of you catch the bug, you can decide then."

WHEN KATE AND PAUL climbed into Paul's pickup to head for home, it was a little past eight. Kate felt invigorated by the exercise and social time. It had helped her forget about the trouble with the Lourdeses for an hour, though as she settled into the passenger seat, the reality quickly returned.

Glancing down, she noticed a message on her cell phone. She hit the button for voice mail and waited for it to connect.

"Who is it?" Paul asked as he wended through the streets of Copper Mill.

Shadows grew long in the quaint town. A few residents were on porches or in their gardens. He reached the turn for Smoky Mountain Road as a voice came on Kate's line. It was Amy Lourdes asking Kate to call her.

Kate called Amy, who immediately picked up.

"The attorney met with Tim today." Amy sounded sad. "He's going to make a motion to allow Tim to stay in the Copper Mill jail instead of transferring him, so that he can be near Jake. It seems to be the best option at this point, since exonerating Tim seems less and less likely. The lawyer told me what they found on the hard drive of Tim's computer . . ."

"And what was that?" Kate said.

"There were e-mails about counterfeiting. As well as encrypted stuff. And scans of bills in different denominations."

Scans of bills. Kate closed her eyes as the statement settled deep. She was trying to free a guilty man!

AMY CALLED AGAIN the next morning just as Kate opened her Bible for her quiet time.

"I'm sorry it's so early . . . It's Jake," the young mother said. She sounded as if she'd been crying. "I'm worried. A fever took root at three o'clock this morning; it's one hundred and one degrees. He's been up all night, hacking and wheezing. If we lived near family, I'd call them, but—"

"Don't apologize. I'm glad you called," Kate said, glancing at her watch. It was six thirty. "I'll be over right away, okay?"

When she arrived at the home, Jake's vapid, lifeless expression and Amy's worried brow told her enough.

"Let's take him to Urgent Care in Pine Ridge," Kate said.

Amy lifted her son effortlessly, attesting to his thin frame and years of ill health. They were at the Pine Ridge Hospital's Urgent Care facility within less than a half hour.

"The fever has me concerned," Dr. McLaughlin, the ER doctor, told Amy and Kate after looking Jake over. He was a handsome man with a shank of dark hair and crow's-feet that added a sense of maturity and wisdom to his look.

"I'm putting him on an IV right away. We can't let him get dehydrated." His brow furrowed as he studied Jake's weary face. "I'd like to admit him. Make sure it doesn't turn into something worse."

Amy turned to Kate. "Tim's arraignment is today. I have to be there."

"You go," Kate assured her. "I'll stay with Jake until you get back."

The young mother's face twisted; she was clearly struggling with what to do.

"I'll be okay, Mom," Jake promised weakly.

"I have your number," Kate assured her. "I can call if there are any changes."

Amy chewed on her lower lip before finally conceding. "The arraignment is at ten."

"It's no problem." Kate touched her shoulder, and Amy inhaled.

"Thank you."

BY NINE THIRTY, Amy was on her way. Kate sat by Jake's bed as he slept and struggled for breath, but the fact that he was sleeping was a good sign. She glanced at her watch. Only five minutes had passed.

She needed access to the computer evidence against Tim. She knew it would help to see those scans and the other files the Secret Service found so incriminating.

Was she indeed trying to free a guilty man? For Amy's

and Jake's sakes she hoped not. She picked up her cell phone and dialed Tim's attorney.

"Lincoln Finch's office," a woman said in a too-deep voice.

It seemed to Kate that with a name like Lincoln Finch, the attorney had been destined to be a lawyer for the down and out.

"Hello, this is Kate Hanlon. I know Mr. Finch is at Tim Lourdes' arraignment," she said. "I heard about the added evidence in the case and wanted to ask some questions about it."

The Lourdeses had previously given the attorney permission to talk with Kate about the case, so she was able to bypass attorney-client confidentiality. She could hear the assistant clicking on a computer keyboard.

The woman breathed deeply, and the alto voice returned. "There were fifteen e-mails to someone named Max Lee regarding counterfeiting," she began. "I can get you the printouts of those. There were also scans on his hard drive."

"Do you have the details on that as well?" Kate asked. "Image resolution, that kind of thing?"

"I do. I'll add copies of that to the file for you. When can you come by?"

"I'm at the hospital with Jake while his mother is at the arraignment."

"I didn't know he was in the hospital. Is everything okay?"

"I'm not sure," Kate said.

"Tell you what, I'll drop these by myself this morning."

KATE HAD THANKED the attorney's assistant effusively when she dropped off the file. Now, as Jake slept, Kate looked through the contents of the thin folder. The e-mails struck her as odd.

Instead of using coded language, Tim wrote openly and frankly about counterfeiting. Messages like "I managed to get those fifties printed off. The alignment was tricky, but they look pretty good. I'll meet you at the Market Street bridge in Chattanooga to make a drop."

Who was this Max Lee? And why would Tim have told him anything about counterfeiting? Was this the accomplice the Secret Service was searching for?

Kate flipped to the information regarding the scanned notes. There was nothing of particular import that she saw, except that the printout looked drastically different from the counterfeit bills she'd seen. The green inks were much brighter in this version, and the fine lines were almost completely obliterated. Something about it felt wrong.

AMY RETURNED AT THREE. "He was indicted," she said simply.

She came to stand alongside Jake's bed. The boy was asleep. A nurse had come at eleven to use the electric clapper on his back. It had been a cruel ordeal to watch, but one that the boy was accustomed to. Now he was as peaceful as a kitten asleep in the sunlight. Amy touched a hand to his brow.

"How are you holding up?" Kate said.

"I keep hoping God will fix all this, but it's just getting worse." She took a deep breath and pulled a chair next to the bed and sat down.

"God is here," Kate assured.

"I do trust him," Amy said, "but we've never gone through anything like this." She searched the ceiling as if she could find answers there.

"Can I pray with you?" Kate offered.

Tears rolled down Amy's cheeks, and she nodded. "I'd like that."

Kate reached for Amy's hand, and the two women bowed their heads. For a moment the only sound in the room was that of Jake breathing in and out, then Kate began. "Father, this family needs you. Jake needs your healing touch. Tim needs wisdom and so does Amy. Help them to find a way through all of this. Work your justice. Send them your love in a tangible way. We know that all things work together for good for those who love you—that is your promise. Amy loves you. So please do what you do best—reveal your compassion to her."

They lifted their faces, and Amy wiped the tears that marked her cheeks.

"What would I do without you here?" she said.

Kate smiled. "God's taking care of you." She turned her head to Jake, who'd awakened. "And him."

BY SATURDAY MORNING, Jake was back home. Kate breathed a sigh of relief when she got the news from Amy.

"They told me to watch him closely, but there was no infection in his lungs."

"Oh, I'm so glad," Kate said.

"I'm going to take him to see Tim again today. He misses his dad."

"Do you need company?"

"Thanks, but we'll be okay. I can sense that prayer of yours already working."

Kate smiled, glad that at least the difficult time was serving to strengthen the young woman's faith.

"Did the lawyer say anything about when Tim could come home? Can he get out on bail?"

"No. He made a motion for bail, but the judge denied it for some reason." Amy sighed. "At this point, I'm just glad he can stay in Copper Mill. Since they have to get the case ready, it sounds like he could be sitting in that jail cell for weeks."

"And . . ." Kate's voice faltered. How could she ask this without sounding nosy? "How are you making ends meet?"

Amy didn't answer at first. "We were having a hard time before. This hasn't exactly helped us."

"Do you have any bills right now that you can't pay?"

Amy paused. "The electric bill is past due."

"You should take the offering money, Amy. The church meant it as a gift for you and Jake as much as for Tim."

"But with this cloud hanging over our heads . . ." Silence followed. "It's just not right," Amy went on. "I believe that God will have to find another way to meet our needs."

Kate frowned. It didn't seem right to ask, but she had to know. "Amy, have you ever heard the name Max Lee?"

"No. Who is that?"

Kate couldn't bring herself to tell Amy that it was the name of the man her husband was apparently in collusion with.

Chapter Thirteen

After they hung up, Kate continued to wonder about Max Lee. How was it that Amy had never even heard the man's name? Was she lying? If so, she was awfully convincing.

Kate pulled out her laptop, setting it up on the kitchen counter to connect to the Internet. While the modem dialed up the number, Kate got a glass of iced tea from the fridge.

When she returned, she punched in her password and was soon searching for the name Max Lee. It was a common enough name. When she typed in the e-mail address from the sheet that Lincoln Finch's assistant had given her, nothing came back in the online white pages. She attempted to send a generic message; it bounced back.

She tried searching for just his name. There were two hundred and seventy-two listings.

So she narrowed it to Max Lee in Tennessee, which seemed reasonable, since Amy had mentioned that they had always lived in the state. This brought the number to a manageable twenty-five. But which one was it?

Kate tapped her fingers on the countertop. She remembered Amy mentioning that they were from Memphis, so she changed the search criteria yet again. One listing. Picking up her cell phone, she dialed the number and waited for an answer.

"Hello." A female voice came on the line.

"Yes . . . um," Kate began, "is there a Max Lee in the house?"

"This is Maxine . . ."

Kate hadn't expected that. "Do you go by Max?"

"No. Who is this?" She sounded young, teenager young.

"Do you know a Tim Lourdes?" she tried.

"Never heard of him."

Kate thanked the woman for her time and hung up. She thought about calling the other twenty-four Max Lees in the state, but decided against it. Even if she could find the one associated with the e-mails, the odds of his spilling it all to Kate weren't on her side. She'd need to take another tack.

EMMA'S ICE CREAM was a favorite hangout in Copper Mill. It was packed with laughing teenagers when Kate and Livvy made their way inside after Livvy got off work on Monday.

The librarian had brought some meals by the Lourdes' home when she'd heard that Jake was back from the hospital on Saturday, and she'd volunteered to help Kate ramp up her sleuthing. Even still, Kate was losing heart. It seemed she was turning over rock after rock only to discover nothing of value. Nothing that the Secret Service hadn't already revealed.

At least they knew where bills were showing up. Perhaps that trail would yield better results.

Seventeen-year-old Anne Jackson was behind the counter. She offered the women a smile. "Hi, Mrs. Hanlon... Mrs. Jenner. How can I help you?"

"Hi, Anne. Is Emma around today?" Kate returned her smile. Over the girl's shoulder, she could see Emma's gray head moving in and out of view through the open doorway.

"I'll get her." Anne turned to speak to her boss.

"That ice cream looks good." Livvy was gazing through the glass case.

Kate's mouth started watering. "I love Emma's mint bonbon," she confessed with a wink.

Just then, Kate heard a teenage boy behind her say, "How can Buck afford a Prowler? Aren't those babies like forty grand?"

Kate turned her head slightly, trying to pick up on what the teens were talking about. He had to mean Buck Lovelace, Millie's son.

"If you lived with your parents all your life, you'd be able to afford hot cars like that too," another answered.

Kate's pulse throbbed.

Finally Emma came out, wiping her hands on a white dishtowel, a curious expression on her face.

"Hello, Kate, Livvy. You needed me?" She wore a yellow dress with tiny pink flowers embroidered along the collar.

"Yes," Kate said, giving Livvy a sly glance. "But first, could we get some cones?"

Emma's face spread into a grin. "Well, of course!"

She bent to scoop them two mint bonbon waffle cones. When they'd paid, Emma said, "From the looks on your faces, I'd say ice cream wasn't the only reason you dropped by." She looked from Kate to Livvy.

"Actually," Kate confessed, "we were wondering if we could ask you a few questions about the counterfeits that passed through here?"

"Well, sure." Emma stopped to scoop herself a cone, then led them to the only empty table in the shop, near the bins of candy that lined the far wall.

The boys at the neighboring table laughed at some joke, apparently having moved on from their prior topic.

The ice cream was rich, decadently fattening. The women sat in comfortable silence as they enjoyed it.

Finally Kate began. "So," she said, "do you know when the counterfeit money showed up?"

Emma squinted her eyes to think. "It was a Friday, about two weeks ago," she confirmed. "Anne was working."

"Was she able to give the authorities a description of the person who passed the bill?" Kate licked her cone just as a drip started trickling down the side.

"You can ask her when she's done with that customer." She nodded toward the girl. "But . . . if you're wondering whether I think it was someone connected to the Lourdes fellow"—she shrugged—"that's hard to say. From what I hear, it sounds like they have an awful lot of evidence against him."

Kate couldn't deny the truth of her words, and yet a part of her still believed the man could be innocent.

"Anne," Emma called to the girl, who'd finished with the customer. She lifted her pretty face. "Can you come here a minute?"

The seventeen-year-old cashier ambled over. "Yes?" she said. She was a lovely young woman with blonde hair and pale blue eyes.

"Kate and Livvy are wondering if you recognized the person who passed the counterfeit money," Emma said.

"Oh." Anne turned to look at each woman, and then she said, "Well, it was a man, two men actually. One was young, the other was older, with white hair."

"Two men? Did anyone else see them other than you?"

Anne shook her head. "I was working the front alone. Brenna was in the back, cleaning the freezer, but she never saw them."

"Have you seen them before in town?" Livvy asked.

"Well, one of them looked like that Tim Lourdes guy, but I admit, I haven't spent a lot of time with him, so I may have that wrong."

"What made you suspect the money was fake?" Kate said.

"It was this weird shade of green, almost blue like they said at that meeting. But it felt like real money, and when I used the counterfeit pen on it, it reacted like real money." She shrugged. "So I accepted it. But I still had this feeling . . . I took it to Emma's that night."

"I knew it was fake,"—Emma picked up the story for her—"especially after I heard about the other bills in town. I called the police right away. Then Sheriff Roberts and that bald Secret Service agent came over to question us."

The story only bolstered the Secret Service's theory that an accomplice was on the loose and that Tim Lourdes was as guilty as sin.

Chapter Fourteen

Kate found "Boom" Lovelace at Bernie's Body Shop on the corner of Sweetwater and Quarry streets. Millie's husband was an ape of a man. He stood over six feet two inches tall, his girth was orbital and his arms hung a bit low.

He was bent under the hood of a baby blue 1963 Chevy Bel Air that was in desperate need of a new coat of paint. Any shine had long since worn away.

She moved next to the vehicle and waited for him to lift his head, but when several minutes passed and he didn't acknowledge her, she finally cleared her throat. "Um . . . excuse me, Boom?"

He banged his head on the metal hood. "Doggone it!" He grabbed the injury and clenched his teeth in a grimace.

"I'm sorry," Kate said, flinching in sympathy.

"How long you been there, Kate?" He rubbed the back of his head.

"I didn't mean to startle you, Boom," she said, glancing around the service bay. There were no other mechanics around, only him and a grease-covered man who took cash in the front office. The place was concrete and steel. A constant wind blew from an oversized fan at the open double-wide garage doors, and an ancient pop machine housed soda at a mere twenty-five cents a can.

"I'm sorry to interrupt your work," she said.

The man waved the apology away and placed dirty hands on his hips. "What can I help you with?" He had kind eyes that sparkled when he talked, even if the rest of him was a bit intimidating.

"Well," Kate said, "I was wondering if I could ask you a couple of questions."

Boom raised his brows and reached for a rag to wipe the black grease from his hands.

"Does this have something to do with Millie's job? She isn't going to get fired, is she?"

"No, nothing like that," Kate assured with a smile. "Actually . . . I wanted to ask you about your vacation. I heard that you all went to Disney on vacation?" Kate tried to sound inquiring without prying.

"Best vacation ever." The man's grin revealed yellowish teeth. "My sons surprised me and Millie with an all-expense-paid trip for the family to Disney World a couple a weeks ago. Well, Millie was over the moon. Has always talked about a vacation to Disney, but we could never do it, even with her workin' two jobs."

"That's wonderful." Kate opted for a positive spin. "Did they win the trip?"

Boom shook his head, chuckling at the idea. "Us Lovelaces aren't exactly what you'd call lucky people. You know those boys, they're always schemin' something." He shook his head. "They've got it in their minds that they can find some get-rich-quick scheme to work for them. They aren't like me." He waved his hand to take in the dingy garage. "I believe in hard work, an honest day's labor. You know?" He turned to Kate, and she nodded her agreement. "Now that Buck has a girlfriend, he's become so . . ." Then he shook his head.

"Have you met her?" Kate asked.

"Nah. Just seen fuzzy pictures. He hasn't brought her around to meet any of us."

Kate started to ask him about it, but he went on. "I don't know what it is with kids these days. They lay around the house all the time, though they sure seem to have enough money to go around."

Chapter Fifteen

Even though it was Saturday, everyone was dressed in their Sunday best, spectators included. The large ballroom's lights were dimmed, save for the spotlights that focused on the competitors at the center of the room. Dancers in flamboyant costumes and heavy makeup performed the Latin dances, Hal and Audrey Harper among them. They moved in perfect symmetry as if attached by invisible cords with every gesture, every step a mirror of their partner.

Kate and Paul had come to Hal and Audrey's competition with Danny and Livvy Jenner. The Cline sisters and Renee Lambert were there too. The seventy-one-year-old woman was dressed in a tight-fitting pink and brown number that would've fit right in on the dance floor, especially with the hot pink manicure and extra-high heels she wore. Thankfully Renee had left her dog Kisses at home. When she'd mentioned bringing the pooch, Audrey had politely informed Renee that she wouldn't get past the front doors with a dog in tow, even a miniature Chihuahua.

Georgia Cline seemed intent on watching the competitors. Even when her sister bent to whisper something in her ear, her gaze didn't leave the floor. It was as if a spell had been cast on her.

"You didn't get Sam to come?" Kate whispered to Renee, who sat on the other side of the Jenners.

The woman whisked her hand as if shooing a fly. "I never should've asked him to be my partner! He's such a party pooper." Someone in back of them shushed her.

"That's too bad," Evelyn Cline said sympathetically. Kate turned to see the man behind them hold a finger to his lips.

The group dance ended, and applause filled the room. There was quiet as the judges tallied scores, then announced the beginning of the individual Latin dances.

Finally a loud, refined-sounding male voice came over the intercom. "Now, dancing the Samba, the husband-and-wife duo, Audrey and Halvard Harper."

The crowd erupted in applause as the couple moved to center stage. Audrey placed her hands in Hal's, and she lifted her face to the side in an almost arrogant pose. A hush fell over the audience. Then the music began, a Brazilian song with a heavy downbeat.

Kate had rarely seen anything so transfixing. Before she knew it, the routine was complete and thunderous applause filled the room. Audrey curtsied while Hal took a step back, then he moved forward and gave a gentlemanly bow. Kate hadn't seen a single flaw. Every motion, every nuance had been perfection on the dance floor. They waved to the crowd, then moved to the judging area to await their scores.

The Cline sisters' mouths had dropped open. Georgia shook her head. "That was amazing," she said. She turned to her sister. "We have to join that competition."

"But we don't have partners," Evelyn squeaked.

Georgia just smiled at her sister.

GEORGIA APPEARED TO BE engrossed in the competition. Renee seemed to enjoy the day, though she didn't say anything about joining the fray herself.

"What do you think?" Kate asked Livvy when they had a free moment. "Will we be entering next time?"

"It's great to watch," she said, "but I'd be Lucille Ball out there." She raised an eyebrow.

When Georgia excused herself to talk to one of the couples, Kate decided to visit with her twin sister.

"Are you going to compete like your sister?" Kate asked as she slid into the seat next to the blue-haired woman.

"Georgia and I do everything together," Evelyn answered in a veiled tone.

"But do you want to?" Kate studied her. "You don't seem as excited about it as she is."

"I've learned that life isn't always about what you want." She smiled when she said it, and there was no malice in her tone, only pure sisterly affection.

Kate saw a blush climb her neck and cheeks.

"Forgive me," she went on. "Georgia has suffered more than her share in her life, so if my entering a dance competition makes her happy"—Evelyn shrugged—"I don't mind that."

Kate wondered what the elder Cline sister had suffered,

but just as she started to ask, Georgia returned. She was huffing in an irritated manner.

"What's wrong?" Evelyn asked her.

"If I'm going to win that prize money, I'm going to have to find a suitable male." Georgia went on. "Well, I haven't been in this position since the Sadie Hawkins dance in tenth grade!"

AFTER LUNCH ON SUNDAY, Kate and Paul went their separate ways, he to read on the back patio and she to work on a stained-glass project. She finished the special order she'd been working on and placed it with a collection of pieces she should have taken to Smith Street Gifts a week ago.

With a frayed scrub brush, she swept tiny shards of glass into a five-gallon bucket she kept near the large worktable. Then she rolled up leftover solder and set them in their bins, which were neatly labeled in her large organizer.

She thought about the dance competition, but mostly she prayed as she worked for the Lourdes family, as well as the various needs in the Faith Briar Church body. She'd been trying to think of a way to approach the Lovelace boys, and she even considered talking to Sheriff Roberts about them. But what evidence did she have? Two seemingly lazy sons who bought cars and took their parents to Disney World? It was hardly search-warrant worthy. All the evidence they did have still pointed to Tim Lourdes.

Kate sent up yet another prayer for Amy, Tim and Jake.

God would take care of the young family's financial needs, she knew, and yet she couldn't help but sense that he wanted her to take a hand in that somehow.

She'd called the local electric company after Amy had mentioned the unpaid bill and asked if it would be possible to pay on their behalf. The woman on the other end of the line had been so touched by the gesture that she'd told Kate the amount. Kate had promptly written a check. And yet the sense that there was more she could do remained. So Kate decided to wait on God and see where he led.

MONDAY MORNING, Kate headed down to the jail to talk to Tim, a plate of fresh-baked cookies in hand. The circles beneath his blue eyes were so dark they seemed tattooed onto his flesh, and the Beach Boys good looks Kate had first noted were gone, replaced by the hollow expression of a man who was lost.

"Mrs. Hanlon." He stood when she and Skip entered the celled area. He'd been sitting on the bed reading a magazine that looked old enough to be from the Ronald Reagan era. "What are you doing here?"

"I thought you could use some company." She handed him the paper plate of plastic-wrap-covered cookies.

Skip unlocked the cell door to let Kate in, then after shutting the door with a clanging sound, he returned to his post. The room smelled stale. "How was your visit with Amy and Jake?" Kate said.

Tim smiled as he bit into one of the tasty treats. "It was good, but I hate that I wasn't able to be there when Jake was in the hospital. He seemed distant to me . . . like I'm losing him." He blew out a heavy breath.

"I'm sorry." Kate patted his shoulder in a motherly way. "I know this has been hard on all of you."

"You've been a good friend." He lifted his face to her. She felt guilty for thinking he might be lying, yet the thought was there. What could she do about it?

"You're innocent," Kate said it as a statement, though she watched his face for any sign of duplicity.

He leaned forward and spoke plainly. "I am."

"Tell me." She sat a bit straighter in the hard chair. "How did encrypted files, e-mails about counterfeiting, and bill scans make it onto your hard drive?"

Tim shook his head. "I don't know. All I can say is that I didn't put them there. I promise you, Kate."

"So who did? Who's Max Lee?" Her tone wasn't accusing, though she knew the questions weren't easy for him.

"I have no idea who he is. I know this all makes me look guilty. The fingerprints were bad enough, but those could be explained away because I work at the bank. This"—he paused, his expression deeply troubled—"I don't have an explanation except the truth. I didn't send any e-mails. I have no idea where or who they come from and I certainly didn't scan any bills. When was I supposed to have time to do this, anyway? My life is full of work, doctor's appointments and taking care of my family. I'm not the kind of person . . ."

Kate held up a hand, and his words fell away. "Did you go to the ice cream shop near the beginning of the month with a gray-haired man?"

Tim shook his head. "Is someone saying I did? I've never been in the place at all. Kate"—he paused and ran a hand through his hair before continuing—"I didn't do this."

"If you didn't do it," Kate said, "somebody did. Maybe there are people who want you to look guilty so the authorities won't suspect them." She paused to let the words sink in, hoping they would strike a chord with Tim somehow. But his expression remained as confused as ever.

"Here's where I'm most confused," Tim said. "Why would I supposedly put fake money in the offering meant for my own family?"

"I don't get it either."

"So then . . . if someone's trying to frame me, who could it be? I don't have any enemies that I know of."

"You can't think of anyone?"

Tim shrugged. "We just moved here; who could have it out for me already? I don't know. And the places the bills are showing up," Tim went on, "aren't places I've ever shopped."

"What does your lawyer say? Has he questioned these witnesses?"

Tim let out a humorless laugh. "All he says is that it doesn't matter, since money circulates and wherever it ends up is just part of the crime. It doesn't mean the person passing it off had anything to do with manufacturing it."

As Kate watched his sincere face, she knew that trust wasn't always earned. Sometimes it was simply given.

Chapter Sixteen

Clifton Beasley sat on the front porch of the Mercantile whittling. The shavings of wood formed a small pool around his feet. The elderly man could often be found there, turning sticks into art. He worked patiently, feeling the wood, sensing what it demanded to yield the piece he'd set out to make. Kate took note to use the same patience in her pursuit of the truth.

Kate and Livvy stood on the sidewalk in the late June heat, not quite ready to go into the store. So far they'd learned that two men were involved in the counterfeiting scheme, one older, one younger.

"But the two Lovelace sons are both in their late twenties . . . ," Livvy said.

Kate shook her head. "Maybe one of them was in disguise?" It came out as a question.

Livvy chewed her lower lip in thought.

The bell above the door made a tinkling sound when Kate and Livvy went inside. It was nearing the supper hour, so the checkout line was long. Several other customers pushed carts up and down aisles. Kate spotted Sam Gorman near the back of the store, a skid of canned goods at his side, where he bent to stock shelves.

"Doing the menial labor, I see," Kate teased as they came up to him.

Sam grinned in his easy way, and he straightened to his full height. "It's my goal to never be above menial labor. Keeps a person humble." He nodded first at Livvy, then at Kate. "Are you looking for something in particular, ladies?"

"We're looking for you, actually," Kate said.

"Oh?" Sam lifted a brow and winked at Livvy. "This isn't about that dance competition, is it?" He shook his head. "Did Renee bribe you to talk me into it? 'Cause I told that woman no already."

Livvy and Kate chuckled.

"You sound undecided." Livvy joined in the teasing. "It'll be fun. I know Danny's thrilled about it."

"You're kidding," he deadpanned, his smile turning into a frown.

"Yes, I'm kidding!" She smiled at Kate. "It's a miracle Danny signed up for lessons. I'm not going to push my luck trying to sign him up for any competition."

Sam shook his head. "Renee's been bugging me constantly, but there's no way. I have two left feet as it is."

"Well," Kate went on, lifting a forefinger, "that's not what we came to see you about. We're wondering what you know about the counterfeit money that was passed here."

Sam pursed his lips.

"Did you see the person who passed the counterfeits?" she went on.

"I didn't. It was late, near closing time. Arlene Jacobs was on duty." He referred to a young woman.

"Did she talk to the Secret Service?" Livvy asked.

Sam nodded. "Arlene came out of that interview scared spitless. She wouldn't tell me a thing about it."

"Why would she be scared?" Kate asked.

"Beats me, but she was white as a sheet."

Had Arlene been threatened or intimidated in any way? "Is she around today?"

Sam glanced at his watch. "She should be up front. Her shift is starting about now."

He led the way to the checkout lane, where Arlene was ringing up cans of cat food for an elderly woman with red fingernails. She turned to bag the goods, then took the woman's money and finished the transaction.

Once the cat lover left, she looked at Sam, then at Kate and Livvy. "Is something wrong?" she asked.

"No," Sam said. "Kate and Livvy were wondering if they could ask you some questions about the counterfeit money." The young woman's face flamed.

"Yes?" She turned to Kate as Kate and Livvy stepped closer so they could talk without the whole store overhearing their conversation.

"Sam said you were frightened when the Secret Service questioned you. Why was that?" Kate started.

Arlene shrugged and crossed her arms in front of her.

Kate tried a new tactic. "What can you tell us about the night you were given the counterfeit bills?"

She tucked her bleached-blonde hair behind her ears, revealing several piercings. "It was at the end of the day," she began in her raspy voice, "so there weren't a lot of customers around. I remember looking at those bills and knowing right away that something wasn't right."

Her gaze flicked to Sam, then back to Kate. "Whoever passed them used real money too."

"How do you know that?" Kate asked.

"There was a real twenty between the two fakes in the till when I looked later." She shrugged. "I wouldn't have swapped them."

"When did you realize they were fake?" Livvy asked.

"Right away, but then the person was right there, and I . . ." She shook her head. "I guess I got nervous about what might happen, so I just took it."

"What did the man look like?" Kate asked.

"Man?" Arlene's face scrunched into puzzlement. "It wasn't a man; it was a woman."

Kate was stunned. A woman? Her mind shot to Amy, then to Millie's assertion that a dark-haired woman had brought the mystery envelope to the church, then to Boom's mention of Buck having a new girlfriend.

"What did she look like?" Livvy asked Arlene.

"Um . . . tall. She had blue eyes and long brown hair."

"Are you sure her hair was brown?" Kate probed.

"It was dark brown and long." Arlene nodded vehemently. "And she had eyeliner, like really thick. But she wasn't Goth or anything, 'cause she was really old."

"How old?"

"Like wrinkled and, I don't know, over forty? I'm not good at guessing that kind of thing."

Kate almost laughed but kept going. "What did the Secret Service say when you told them that?"

"Nothin'. They mostly took notes and acted like I was a liar." Another customer came to her checkout lane, and she hesitated before saying, "Was there anything else?"

Kate said, "No. This has been extremely helpful."

They excused themselves and went outside, where the heat had not abated. Neither had the questions.

KATE WALKED LIVVY to the library, where she'd left her car, then drove to her quiet house. Paul was at a community ministerial meeting for the evening, so she got supper going for herself. She wasn't particularly hungry, so she grabbed bread and deli meat for a sandwich. As she spread mayonnaise on a slice, her mind twisted in thought.

Two men and a woman? If there was more than one accomplice, why hadn't the Secret Service arrested anyone else? Amy didn't fit the description—at least not as to the age, though she did have blue eyes and long brown hair.

She picked up the phone to dial Amy in hopes that Tim's lawyer had some new information, but there was no answer. She hung up before the answering machine finished its greeting.

Cutting her sandwich in half, she took a bite. Then, picking up the phone again, she dialed the deputy's office, hoping Skip Spencer was still on duty.

The officer answered on the third ring. "Deputy Spencer."

"Skip," Kate began.

"Mrs. Hanlon," he said in his friendly tone.

"Has Tim Lourdes had any visitors other than Amy and Jake?"

"Not besides the two of them and you and Mr. Hanlon. And his lawyer, of course."

There was the sound of voices in the background then, and Skip talking to whoever it was.

The next voice Kate heard was that of Secret Service Agent Norris, the blond Tom Cruise she'd run into several times.

"Mrs. Hanlon?" he said into the phone. "Please be clear that this is a federal matter."

"Uh," Kate began, "yes, sir."

"Our ongoing investigation is none of your concern. Do you understand that? We will share all of our findings with Mr. Lourdes' attorney."

Then the agent hung up on her.

Chapter Seventeen

Kate stared at the phone as shock settled over her. She knew the man had a job to do, and yet a sense of injustice tugged at her. She'd merely asked if Tim had visitors; how had that impeded his investigation?

"Father," a prayer welled up in her, "am I doing the right thing? Or am I being played for a fool?"

Isaiah 1:17 pressed itself into her thoughts, so she rose to look up the verse, though she thought that she already knew what it said. *Learn to do good. Seek justice. Help the oppressed. Defend the cause of orphans. Fight for the rights of widows.*

She inhaled and lifted her face to the ceiling. As much as Amy and Tim had asked for her help, she felt strongly that God had asked this of her. He was in charge of the outcome. It was simply her task to follow his lead.

He would point her to the truth, whatever that was. Whoever had committed the crime, God knew his, or her, name.

When Kate saw Amy Lourdes the next morning, the young woman was just getting into her car, a faded yellow subcompact that had spots of rust emerging on its hood.

"Oh, Kate," Amy said, "I was going to call you. I saw your number on caller ID last night. I'm sorry I didn't get back to you. I was meeting with Tim's lawyer."

"What did he say?" Kate came up alongside her and noticed Jake seated in the passenger's seat and fidgeting with the knobs on the radio.

"Other than that they're looking for accomplices, not much." She lifted her eyes to Kate, fear in the lines of her face. "Just that he isn't real hopeful about Tim's case."

Amy was looking at her watch, and for the first time Kate realized the young mother was dressed up.

"Were you headed somewhere?" Kate asked.

"Doctor's visit for Jake—just a follow-up. And then a job interview for me."

"A job interview? Where?"

"It's at the Hamilton Springs Hotel. And honestly, I don't know how I'll manage while still homeschooling Jake, but things are just too tight financially for me to see any other options. From the way the lawyer talked last night, it's going to be a long time before Tim's case even goes to trial, and we'll lose everything if I don't do something." She paused and added, "Thank you, by the way, for paying the electric bill."

"How did you know?"

"I have my sources." She smiled, and Kate could see that she was deeply moved by the gesture.

"Would you like me to watch Jake for you? During your interview?"

"Thank you." Amy shook her head. "Another time, maybe." She paused, offering a smile to her son. "You'll be a good boy, won't you?"

Jake nodded and smiled at his mother.

"If I don't get the job today, I'll call." She put on a smile, obviously trying to be brave.

"Let me know how it goes, okay?" Kate asked.

Amy nodded and backed out of the driveway.

BETTY'S BEAUTY PARLOR was where many of the women in Copper Mill went to have their hair done. Kate was no exception. She made her way to the small downtown storefront and took a seat on the bench in the waiting area. Betty lifted her bleached-blonde head and waved at her from her station in front of the wall of mirrors. Alicia and Ronda, the two other stylists, chatted with their clients.

The shop was early 1960s vintage, with padded benches and salmon-colored adjustable vinyl chairs. The floor was a white-and-aqua checkerboard, and posters of blonde Doris Day wannabes hung on the walls, their backgrounds faded to a pale puce color. The scent of perm solution hung in the air.

Kate paged through a fashion magazine, though her thoughts were elsewhere. She hoped someone in the busy shop would have answers for her many questions.

Finally, Betty's customer got up to pay, and Betty waved Kate over to her station. She fitted a large plastic bib across Kate's front, fastening it behind her neck.

"What were we thinking today?" she asked. "Maybe try a new look? We could go ultra short and red?"

Kate laughed at the image. "Thanks, but I'll stick with a trim and touch-up."

"Okeydoke."

Betty moved to the back to mix up Kate's dye, then returned a few minutes later with a plastic cup and brush in hand. "So how have you been? I feel as if I haven't seen you in ages."

She ran a comb through Kate's shoulder-length hair and spoke to her in the mirror. "I've been keeping busy," Kate said. "Helping out with Jake and Amy Lourdes."

The woman at the next station made a sound of disgust, and Kate turned to her, surprised by the outburst.

"It's a sorry day when people have to resort to counterfeiting," the woman said, making no apology for her eruption.

Ire rose within Kate. This woman didn't know Tim or Amy, and yet she'd found him guilty in her inner courtroom. Kate bit her tongue and waited until the woman was done with her hairdressing before venturing into conversation again.

"Everyone's on edge," Betty said quietly to Kate, probably sensing Kate's sudden mood shift. She moved around Kate's head as she brushed her hair. "*Someone* needs to help Amy and Jake in the midst of this, and I'm glad you're there for them."

"Thanks, Betty." Kate prepared to change subjects, careful not to sound as if she was fishing for gossip. "Do you know the Lovelace boys?"

"Millie's sons?"

Kate nodded.

"Not a whole lot, other than that they don't get out much. I did hear that Buck has a girlfriend." Betty began to brush on the hair dye, starting at the roots and working down Kate's head. "And I know those two do a lot with computers."

She moved to the other side of Kate's head.

"What exactly do they do with computers?" Kate's mind began to spin.

"My nephew graduated with them. He said they're geniuses when it comes to that stuff. Programming, all of that."

"*Hmm.*" Kate let the information simmer.

"Oh yes. He said if the Lovelace boys wanted to hack into FBI files, he wouldn't put it past them. They're that good."

"PLACE YOUR HAND HERE," Audrey told Paul that night at dance class. She placed Paul's right hand firmly on Kate's waist. "And be in control. Don't let her lead." Audrey nodded to Kate.

"You have to understand, this is a long-standing problem with us," Paul quipped.

Kate swatted him playfully on the arm. "Hey!"

"You see what I mean?" Paul feigned a wounded arm.

Hal came up behind his wife, a smirk on his face. "Audrey can be like that at home too," he said.

Audrey turned and put her hands on her hips.

They laughed, and Kate noted how the couple treated each other with affection. Not like a couple who'd been married years and years and took each other for granted, but like a couple still deeply in love.

Paul gave her a wink. Heat flooded her, and she squeezed his hand.

"You're doing very well," Audrey encouraged as she moved on to the next pair.

As Kate studied Audrey and Hal, she realized that she and Paul got along well with them. There was a camaraderie whenever they were together that she found enjoyable.

After the others had left when class was finished, Kate and Paul waited for Audrey and Hal near the piano. Audrey lifted her robin's egg eyes to Kate, the corners crinkling in familiar lines.

"We were wondering if the two of you would like to have supper together some night," Kate said when Audrey came over. "We know how hard it can be to make friends in a new town."

"Oh, that's so sweet of you," Audrey said, fluttering a ring-encrusted hand to her chest. Hal offered one of his agreeable nods, and she said, "When were you thinking?"

"Well I have choir tomorrow night and, of course, dance on Thursday, so how does Friday look for you?"

"Perfect!"

THERE HAD BEEN NO JOB OFFER for Amy Lourdes on Tuesday or the following days that week, though the authorities also hadn't shown up at her door with accusations of her collusion in the counterfeiting scheme either. So Kate supposed that was a silver lining—but not much of one.

Amy had several interviews on the following days as well, including that Friday afternoon, and Kate stayed with Jake to make things easier on her.

Kate was watching a children's television show with Jake, who had fallen asleep on the couch, when the front door opened, then banged shut. Kate saw the strain on Amy's face.

"What's wrong?" She moved over to the young mother.

Amy sighed and shook her head. "I didn't expect the rumors," she said in a low voice.

"Rumors?"

"It seems no one wants to hire the wife of a counterfeiter. Did Tim tell you that the bank fired him?"

Kate shook her head.

"They didn't even bother calling. I got a letter in the mail." She held up the white sheet of paper.

A mere paragraph in length, it read,

Dear Tim,

Given the pending investigation and trial, we have decided to terminate your employment, effective immediately. The charges of counterfeiting are serious and could hurt the reputation of the bank; therefore, we feel we have no other recourse. Since this falls under the category of "termination for cause," there are no unemployment benefits available to you.

Melvin McKinney
Manager, Mid-Cumberland Bank and Trust

"I don't know what I can do," Amy said when Kate handed the letter back. A shimmer of tears slipped down her cheek. "If we can't keep up our health insurance premiums . . ."

Kate didn't know what to say but tried to comfort the young woman with a hand on her back. Though she knew that without the funds to pay for their essential needs, such as their rent and health insurance, the mother and son might well be on a path to complete devastation.

Chapter Eighteen

Kate made it home, slipped into clothes for supper and was in the car by six o'clock with Paul by her side.

After Amy had calmed down, Kate had assured her that God had not forgotten her family. And there were good-hearted people at Faith Briar, dear people who would give their all for someone in need. Amy simply needed proof of it.

"Did the Harpers say why we couldn't just meet at the Bristol?" Paul asked, pulling Kate's attention to the present.

"Audrey wanted to show me the house now that she's all settled and decorated." She smiled at him. "It's a girl thing. Besides, it's always good to carpool."

THE ENTRANCE TO THE HARPERS' winding driveway was surrounded by lush flower beds and a well-groomed lawn. The cobbled drive wound amid ferns and thick deciduous trees until the view of misty ridges and valleys opened up beyond. Then the house came into sight. A stone structure with banks of windows trimmed in white, it looked as though it had been there for centuries, kept pristine by each successive generation.

Audrey was in the front yard when they approached the house. She bent to pick weeds, then straightened as a broad smile filled her face. Paul pulled up in front of the three-car garage, where a Town Car and a vintage Porsche were parked in front of the closed doors.

"I'm sorry, but if I see a weed, I have to pull it," Audrey said, holding up the plants in her hands, though she was attired in a nice dress for supper. She tossed them to the side and wiped the dirt from her hands. "I'm so glad you made it."

Kate and Paul got out of the car and admired the colorful flower beds.

"Want to come see the house?" Audrey tilted her head toward the lovely home.

The Hanlons followed her as she moved through the front door and into the entryway.

"You're our first visitors," Audrey said, gesturing toward a staircase that wound to the second story. A chandelier overhead sparkled on the hardwood floors. The walls were a distinguished shade of mauve, lending to the sense of refinement.

"Every wall was covered in wallpaper when we moved in," Audrey said with a laugh. "Took me a very long day to get it all off."

She moved down the hall toward the back of the house, where the darling kitchen with granite countertops and maple cabinetry gleamed.

Turning on the water, Audrey washed her hands, drying

them on a kitchen towel. "Hal and I had the kitchen redone. The laundry room is back there." She motioned toward a room off the back of the house, flanking the back of the garage.

"This is beautiful," Kate commented, taking in the vista beyond the bank of windows that overlooked hazy-blue mountains and valleys. A dining room and great room spread toward the north, a single space with each area defined by changes in flooring. Every piece of furniture seemed suited to Audrey's flamboyant yet classical sensibilities.

"Come." She led the way back to the entry. "The library and formal dining room are down here too." These rooms flanked the front of the house. Floor-to-ceiling book shelves made up the walls of the library with a rolling ladder attached to the top of the shelving. The oversized coffee table held numerous periodicals; Kate noted dance magazines as well as financial digests. One wall held a glass case filled with dancing trophies. Kate bent to study the inscriptions. While some were for specific dances, many read "Latin Rhythm Champion."

The upstairs was equally lovely, with three guest bedrooms and sweeping views.

"This is the Paso Doble Room," Audrey said of one bedroom with burnt red walls and a Latin feel, its focal point a painting of a matador with cape extended.

"That's impressive," Kate said.

"Thank you. That's one of my originals."

Kate moved to study it closer. The use of color and texture was outstanding, especially for a watercolor. "You did this?"

Audrey nodded. "After dance, painting is my next love."

"How do you find time to do all this?" Kate asked.

Paul's mouth hung open in obvious awe.

Audrey shrugged. "It's a hobby, just like dancing. I love it."

"Could I hire you to decorate my place?" Kate kidded.

Her worn-out rambler had grown on her, with its tiny, outdated kitchen and foggy-glassed patio door. Something about it said "home" even though it was far from perfect like this place was.

Paul's expression said, *We can't afford this on a pastor's salary!*

When the group walked outside, Hal was just coming from the side door of the garage. He wiped his hands on a shop rag.

"The garage is still a wreck," Audrey said, nodding toward the three-car garage with carriage-house doors. "That's where Hal keeps all his man stuff." She waved a hand. "Boring." She smiled, then turned to her husband. "Are you almost ready to go?"

"In a minute," Hal said. "Let me wash up."

He disappeared into the house and returned a few moments later, scrubbed and ready. They climbed into the Town Car and roared toward the Bristol.

THE BRISTOL RESTAURANT was inside the Hamilton Springs Hotel. The Hanlons and the Harpers made their way inside the wide double doors that opened onto a massive foyer with double staircases that wound their way up to the floors above.

The restaurant was to the left of the foyer. A tall waiter led them to a table for four alongside a bank of divided windows overlooking a pond. Ducks swam across the glassy surface, and Kate could see children with fishing poles at the ready along its shores.

Audrey sighed contentedly as the waiter handed them their menus and left to get their beverages.

"This is a great idea." She looked at her husband. "Hal is much more introverted than I am, so moving to a new town and making friends isn't as big a deal to him. But for me . . . I just need that connection more." She splayed a hand across her throat.

"I'm the same way," Kate said. "It's important to find friends wherever you live."

"The dance studio has been good for that too," Audrey added.

Hal set his menu down and smiled at his wife.

"Where did you say you worked before?" Paul asked Hal, his blue eyes alight with interest.

"I was a broker in New York."

"He was a *top-selling* broker," Audrey added. "He broke a million dollars in profits when he was just twenty-four." She glowed with pride at her husband.

"How long did you do that?" Kate asked.

"Let's see . . . Well, I was in New York for thirty years. So about that long. It was a livin'."

The way he said *livin'* reminded Kate of Texas. There was a hint of a twang at the end of the word.

"Have you ever lived in the South?" she asked.

Hal paused for a moment as if the question surprised him, then he smiled. "How did you guess that? I spent my growin'-up years in Fort Worth, and a few years shortly after we married."

"I recognized a bit of the twang in your voice. I was born and raised there, and we lived in San Antonio for many years before coming here."

"No kidding?" Audrey seemed delighted at the coincidence. "We have a lot of friends and family back there. How about you?"

"Friends," Kate said. "And some extended family on my side, but Paul's family was from this area. Our children have scattered to the winds."

The waiter arrived with their drinks and took their food orders, then scooted to the next table.

"How many children do you have?" Audrey asked.

Kate and Paul told them about their three grown children—Andrew, a married real estate attorney in Philadelphia, with two kids of his own; Melissa, also married with a baby daughter, in Atlanta; and Rebecca, the youngest Hanlon offspring, who was single and living in New York City, doing her best to break through as an actress on Broadway.

Audrey's expression sobered. "We weren't able to have children. I guess that's why the dance studio is so important to me. I get to teach children as well as adults."

How different life would've been if Kate and Paul hadn't had children, she thought. Would they have made the same choices, lived in the same places? No doubt such a reality would have changed every aspect of their lives and their marriage.

Their meals arrived—scallops and red snapper, prime rib

and linguini. The scent was intoxicating, and the table fell silent as everyone dug in.

It was Hal who broke the silence. "So what's happening with that fellow from church? The one that was arrested?" He sliced a piece of rare prime rib as he spoke.

"It's devastating, really," Paul began. "Their son Jake has spent his short life in and out of hospitals. And now this . . . The authorities say there's enough evidence to convict Tim."

"Tim's wife and son are the ones who are really taking the brunt," Kate added. "The bank fired Tim, and Amy's looking for jobs. Without his income, I don't know what they'll do."

"Has she had any luck?" Audrey asked.

Kate shook her head.

Audrey sat back in thought, then her face lit in a smile. "Maybe we could hire her to help at the studio." She turned toward her husband for affirmation. "She could answer phones, sign up new enrollees, clean a little."

"That would be amazing," Kate said.

"It wouldn't be enough to cover all their costs, I'm sure," Audrey went on. "But it could help. I'll call her first thing in the morning."

When the bill arrived, Hal reached for it immediately.

"As I recall, we were the ones who invited you," Paul said.

"I know how much pastors make," Hal said without a hint of arrogance in his voice.

AS THEY DROVE BACK to the Harpers' to pick up Kate's car, the sounds of gentle jazz flowing from the radio, Audrey said, "Have you made up your minds about entering the beginners' competition? The deadline for signing up is this week."

"I don't know . . . ," Paul said.

"But seeing other beginners out there will give you a boost of confidence," Audrey said. She turned in her seat to look at them. "That's really the whole point of the competition, you know. It will help you to see that compared to other beginners, you two really are good. I see a lot of potential in you. You know the Cline sisters are competing, don't you?"

"Have they found partners?" Paul asked.

"No. They've been working up routines with Hal for now. Of course, as an instructor, he isn't permitted to compete in the competition, so they'll have to find partners soon."

"What will they do if they can't find partners?" Paul asked.

"Have you met those two women?" Audrey said, "I have no doubt they'll be able to persuade someone to join them."

"What do you think?" Kate turned to Paul. "It might be fun."

"Oh, all right," he conceded. "But no photographs. The last thing I need is to have something like that circulating in the *Copper Mill Chronicle*."

Chapter Nineteen

"Thank you!" Amy chirped when Kate answered the phone the next day. The excitement in her voice was unmistakable.

"What did I do?" Kate wiped the flour from her hands. She'd been baking cinnamon buns when the phone had rung.

"You found me a job at the dance studio! And it's perfect. It's really flexible. I'll even be able to keep homeschooling Jake in the back room while I answer phones and clean."

"I'm so glad for you," Kate said. "It was all Audrey's idea."

"Well, if you hadn't mentioned that I was looking, I wouldn't have gotten it. I can't thank you enough," she said. It was good to hear joy in her voice.

AS KATE MADE BREAKFAST Saturday morning, she thought of a question that had yet to be answered. By that afternoon, she and Livvy had printed out directions and were headed to one of the big computer stores in Chattanooga.

"So what exactly are we doing again?" Livvy asked, switching into the left lane.

"I was doing a bit more research on that scanner they took from Tim's house," Kate explained, looking out the passenger-side window of Livvy's SUV. "It seems the manufacturer installed anticounterfeit devices on it at the factory."

"Meaning what?" Livvy said, glancing at her as she made a turn.

"Meaning that at least when it was new, Tim Lourdes' scanner was built to detect if someone was attempting to reproduce money, and it would automatically halt the activity. It even had built-in reporting systems."

"It would e-mail the authorities?" Livvy said as if she couldn't fathom such a thing. "Software that tells the police if illegal activities are afoot? Talk about Big Brother!"

Kate smiled. "And that's on a standard scanner!" She paused. "Just think about what a high-end scanner would do. It means it would be all the harder for the scans to end up on Tim's system. Things just don't add up."

"Could he have overwritten the software, hacked into it somehow? Or used a different scanner?" Livvy asked as she drove.

"That's the question, isn't it?"

THE COMPUTER STORE was on Gunbarrel Road, a name Kate found to be completely ironic given the nature of their visit. A red-vested employee met them at the door.

"Can I help you ladies?" the young man with curly bright red hair said.

"I don't know," Kate began. "We have some questions about a particular scanner and printer."

"Sure." He led them to the computer section of the store, then stood expectantly, as if waiting for them to pick out a brand and model.

"We aren't in the market to buy them," Kate explained.

His face scrunched in confusion.

"We're actually doing some research on a counterfeit money operation," Livvy clarified.

The man's confusion only increased.

Kate cleared her throat. "We're not looking to make . . . I mean . . ." She wasn't sure how to word it. "Maybe the people we need are on your technology assistance team."

Relief filled his face. "Right over here." He pointed them to the customer service counter to their left.

Kate managed to explain the situation to the technician, a dark-haired young man with a deep cleft in his chin.

"What was the model?" he asked, running his fingers through unruly hair.

Kate handed him the user's guide with all the details on Tim's scanner and printer. He studied it for a moment before bringing the information up on his monitor. Then he punched in the Web site Kate mentioned that dealt with the specifications on counterfeiting.

"I saw on one of your sites," Kate said while the man read, "that some scanners have built-in safeguards to keep people from scanning and reproducing money."

He nodded absently. "ACDs—anticounterfeiting devices. Not all have them, but a few brands do." He clicked around on his computer screen. "This is one of them, though." He nodded again, repeating essentially what Kate had told Livvy about the scanners on the drive to Chattanooga.

He clicked around on the screen for a few more minutes. "That's interesting," he said.

"What?" Kate stretched to see the screen.

"Take a look at this." He turned the monitor so Kate and Livvy could have a better look. "The dpi—or dots per inch—that this particular printer is capable of . . . Well, let's just say your money would've looked like mud compared to a real dollar bill if it was printed on that printer."

KATE CALLED AMY when they were minutes outside of Copper Mill. She held the printouts the IT expert had given her regarding the scanning and printing capabilities of Tim's hardware in her lap. He'd made extra copies so Kate could give a set to Tim's attorney.

"I think we have enough to get Tim off," Kate said to Amy.

"How?"

Kate explained everything she'd learned about the dpi limitations of Tim's printer and the anticounterfeiting device on the scanner.

"That's great." But instead of sounding pleased, Amy sounded deflated.

"What's wrong? I thought you'd be happy," Kate said.

"I just got a call from Tim's lawyer. The Secret Service has uncovered some sort of print shop."

A metal ball sank in Kate's stomach. "Where?"

"I'm headed out the door to go there right now. It's in a storage facility outside of town, rented in Tim's name. He didn't do this, Kate. I know it looks really bad. But someone is setting him up. I promise you."

Kate wasn't sure what to believe anymore.

By the time Kate and Livvy made it to the address, Amy was there. The door to the facility was closed, though four men stood out front talking, including agents Norris and Wimper; Tim's attorney, Lincoln Finch; and the district attorney whom Kate recognized from past cases.

The SUV's tires crunched on gravel as Livvy parked alongside the agents' dark sedan. The women got out, and the men nodded in acknowledgment. Kate could see that Jake was asleep in Amy's car.

Lincoln Finch came up alongside Kate, Livvy and Amy. "This doesn't look good."

"What did they find?" Amy got to the point. Her forehead wrinkled, and her face was strained.

"A smoking gun," the agent said from behind them. "There's a full print shop in there." He pointed with pursed lips.

"How did they connect this to Tim?" Kate asked.

"Other than his signature being on the storage lease, dated two months ago?" Finch said.

"Do you have a copy of the contract?" Amy asked Finch. He handed her the paperwork, which she shuffled through.

"Wait," Amy said, her face scrunched. "This isn't Tim's signature." Her voice was angry. She shoved the paper toward the man and pointed at the signature line.

"We'll get an analysis on that signature," the lawyer said calmly to Amy as he took the document.

Kate wondered why the Secret Service hadn't checked the signature and then looked directly at Finch and said, "The equipment they seized—the scanner, printer and computer—it isn't capable of the things they're saying he did. It even had ACDs preprogrammed into it. There wasn't a ream of paper in the house, much less the expensive rag paper he would've needed to create the bills—"

"This print shop pretty much makes that irrelevant, Mrs. Hanlon," Agent Norris interrupted. "I recommend that you leave the investigating to the authorities. Take a look at that print shop in there; it's full of Tim Lourdes' stuff."

Chapter Twenty

Kate and Paul met the Cline sisters at the studio for their competition practice, a now-daily event between the hours of seven and eight o'clock in the morning, at least that week. With the contest coming up in just under four weeks, they needed to get a routine down. Amy waved at them as they practiced, then she disappeared into the back room.

Paul seemed frustrated, though Kate had to admit he was a trooper. If he missed a step, he'd smile and shrug his shoulders, then carry on.

The dance Audrey had chosen for them was the Viennese waltz, one of the most classic styles. While the dance looked simple enough, with its up-and-down glides across the floor, it required a level of concentration Kate hadn't had to call on since she'd first taken up stained-glass work.

Kate stood tall, back straight, as Paul led her into the quick-paced pattern. Meanwhile, Hal was practicing with each of the Cline sisters in turn. He took Evelyn in his arms and went through the routine as Georgia looked on.

"You're running out of time," Audrey was saying from across the room. "Your partners won't have time to memorize the routine if you don't choose them soon."

"We've asked every male in Copper Mill." Georgia turned to her, frustration etched in the lines of her face.

"Maybe you're not looking in the right places," Audrey returned. "You should go where people are already dancing, like the VFW."

The music stopped, so Kate and Paul took a break, going to stand with the irked twin.

"Of course, I know we need to find partners," she was saying under her breath. "I've been looking!" She turned to Kate. "This is so important to Evelyn. Of course I've been looking."

Kate tilted her head. "This is important to Evelyn?" she said, surprised at the younger twin's change of heart. Hadn't Evelyn said she was dancing to please Georgia?

"When we were younger . . ." Georgia clasped a hand to her chest as she spoke. Evelyn and Hal were working through a tricky turn on the other side of the room. "Our mother signed us up for dance. For five years we studied."

She glanced at her sister and Hal as she whispered. "Evelyn was quite good too, and devoted, but her partner, a young man whom she was quite smitten with, left her for a tap dancer. It was devastating! Poor Evelyn hasn't danced again until now. So, you see, this is a monumental step for her, a chance for her to put the past behind her!"

"If you can find partners," Paul added.

"Exactly."

HOW HAVE I BEEN wrangled into this? Kate thought as she, Evelyn and Georgia Cline entered the depths of the Pine Ridge VFW.

Housed in a gray cinder block building, the VFW smelled both musty and smoky. The front door was padded burgundy vinyl with a small diamond-shaped window carved into its top, and the interior of the place fit its introduction. With wood paneling, green carpet and orange vinyl booths, the VFW was straight out of the seventies. The word *Naugahyde* came to mind.

"Where do you want to sit?" Evelyn asked Kate.

Kate shrugged. "Anywhere is fine. I'm just here to provide moral support."

Georgia was in the lead, not looking back once to see if they followed. She took them straight to the tables that surrounded the dance floor, where several gray-haired couples were waltzing. Each took a chair, and Georgia craned her neck to glance around. A teenage girl with braces on her teeth and pigtails that rode high on each side of her head stopped at the table to take their soda orders, then moved to the next table.

"So what do we do?" Evelyn asked. She kept her hand in front of her face and her head tilted toward the floor as if she were trying to hide.

"Don't ask me. It's been a long time since I've been out looking for a date," Kate said.

"We're *not* looking for dates!" Georgia protested, her blue hair jiggling as she shook her head. "We're looking for dance partners. We have to make that clear from the start. We don't need that monkey business."

She chuckled, her eyes drifting over the other tables. Most of the customers were gray or bald, though there were a couple of younger men. But even they looked to be in their fifties.

"Why did you want me to come again?" Kate asked Georgia.

The blue-haired bank teller gazed at Kate for a moment before answering, and when she did talk, it was in a slightly condescending tone. "You're a pastor's wife, Kate."

"I know that." Kate grinned. "That's why it seems a bit unusual, don't you think?"

"Well, if people see that you're with us, we'll be less likely to attract the wrong kind of men."

Kate laughed a bit too loudly. Several heads turned toward her, so she lowered her voice. "So I'm your security blanket?"

"It's not funny." Georgia kept a straight face. Then she pointed. "Is that who I think it is?"

There on the dance floor doing the cha-cha under the disco ball's flickering lights was Joe Tucker, a faithful member of Faith Briar Church. Because he usually walked with a cane, the sight was more than surprising.

Instead of the awkward movements Kate would have expected, the music seemed to transport the man and give him a sort of elegance. He still used the cane as he moved, of course, but it struck Kate as something Fred Astaire would have done in one of his movies to make the performance that much more entertaining. Kate's jaw dropped as she watched the woodsman move through the complicated dance.

When he finished, he and his petite gray-haired partner moved to a table at the opposite side of the polished floor where another couple sat. At first Kate didn't recognize them either, though something seemed familiar about the man. He had a long gray beard that reached halfway down his belly. Then she realized the man was her mail carrier. The only name she knew him by was Fish.

"That's Joe Tucker, isn't it?" Georgia was asking of Joe.

Kate nodded, still speechless. Finally she managed, "I had no idea he was a dancer."

"Well, he looks like a perfect candidate to me." Georgia was on her feet.

"He *has* a date," Evelyn cautioned, drawing her sister's attention back to their table as she pointed to Joe's partner.

Georgia shrugged. "I'm just going to say hello." She tugged Kate to her feet. "Kate, come with me. We'll see if that other fellow will dance with Evelyn too."

Kate was mortified. "You're going to ask my mailman to be in your dance competition?"

Georgia clapped her hands together as she grinned. "It's perfect. We can kill two birds as it were."

She looked at her sister meaningfully, and Evelyn rose to her feet. She tugged her blouse down and touched her blue hair as if to make sure every strand was in place. The long-bearded man lifted curious eyes.

"Are you sure?" she said, her brows coming together in doubt.

"If he can dance, let's give him a whirl." Georgia marched across the floor to the other table, almost knocking over several couples in the process. Kate and Evelyn followed at a more cautious pace.

Georgia waited, tapping her foot as she stood on the side. Then she followed as Kate took them to Joe's table. He sipped a glass of water and leaned toward his dance partner in conversation. Kate wondered who the pretty woman could be.

He lifted his head and recognition lit his face. "Kate. What are you doing here?"

"I . . . uh." She had no idea how to answer the question.

"Hello, Joe." Georgia stuck a hand out to Joe.

Joe said hello, then acknowledged Evelyn, who stood behind Kate.

"You were cutting a mean rug out there," Georgia said.

The woman didn't waste time, did she? Joe's partner smirked at the comment.

"Oh . . . uh." Joe cleared his throat and sat back in his seat. "This is my sister Marie. She lives here in Pine Ridge." He motioned to his dance partner, then to their friends across the table. "And you know Fish and his friend Angel Martins."

On the word *friend*, Evelyn's shoulders drooped.

"So . . . ," Marie said, her pale green eyes on Georgia, "it's nice of you to say hello." An awkward silence fell.

Finally Georgia pinned her gaze on Joe and said, "Would you like to dance?"

His bushy white eyebrows shot up, and he turned to Kate. She hated being in the midst of an ambush, but she had to admit it was a bit fun to watch Joe squirm. Kate shrugged as if in answer to an unspoken question. Then he turned to his sister, whose face took on a full grin.

"It's fine with me," Marie said. "How often do I get to see my seventy-year-old brother out with a new girl?"

Joe shot her a "Watch it, Sis!" look as he got to his feet and led Georgia to the floor.

"I haven't seen you here before," Fish said to Kate.

Whenever Kate had talked to the mailman before, she was usually staring at his long beard; she hadn't noticed what penetrating eyes he had.

"I don't usually come here," Kate said with a smile.

"You're a dancer too, Mrs. Hanlon?" Marie asked.

"She's excellent," Evelyn said. "She and Pastor Hanlon are participating in a dance competition with us."

Kate felt a blush heat her face. "Well, that's kind of you, Evelyn. I wouldn't say we're excellent, but we do enjoy ourselves. Well, I enjoy myself, and Paul humors me."

Joe and Georgia returned to the table. Joe had an oddly pleased expression on his face. He sat next to Fish and said something into his ear. The bearded mailman smiled at Evelyn, then turned to Joe before whispering something. Georgia nodded enthusiastically.

Then she said, "Joe's going to do it!"

Kate couldn't believe her ears. "How did you manage that?"

Joe cut in. "It's one of those things I've always secretly wanted to do. And Fish here just agreed to be your partner too, Evelyn."

"Really?" Evelyn pulled a hand over her mouth, and for a moment Kate thought she might cry.

Chapter Twenty-One

Amy and Jake met Kate for lunch on Tuesday at the Country Diner after their daily visit with Tim. The young woman seemed subdued, watching her son's every move.

Jake scooted into the seat alongside his mother. He began coughing and wheezing almost as soon as he was seated. He held a small hand over his mouth, and Amy patted him firmly on the back, but when the bout wouldn't cease, she got out his asthma inhaler and placed it on his mouth. He closed his eyes and breathed in the medicated puff.

"He's been sick again," she said. She stroked his hair. "Last night he was up a good three hours."

Jake puckered his lips in obvious frustration.

"Have you heard anything more on Tim's case?" Kate asked in a low voice.

Amy opened her mouth as if to speak, but then LuAnne came up to the table. The heavyset woman smiled at Jake.

"Hey, buddy," she said, bending down to meet his eyes. "What's wrong?"

The sympathy was more than the boy could bear. Tears burst from him, and he covered his face with his hands. Amy pulled him into a hug.

LuAnne stood upright and mouthed "I'm sorry" to Amy. The young mother smiled as she shook her head.

Then she mouthed back "He'll be okay" before stating, "Two root beers for us. And let's get Jake some chicken nuggets." Then she ordered a Reuben with Thousand Island dressing for herself.

"I'll take the same," Kate said, offering a gentle smile before LuAnne left to place the order.

"He misses Tim." Amy closed her eyes. "When we went to see him this morning, he was beside himself. Jail is hard on Tim. He was pacing the cell like one of those animals at the zoo. It scared Jake. I worry about both of them, Kate." Tears glistened on her cheeks. "This is tearing us apart."

"I'm sorry."

"I wish we'd never moved here," Amy said.

Kate felt her pain. Being alone in a new place, feeling watched, judged. She was trying so hard to be brave. A lot of people would have given up a long time ago if they'd been in the same situation.

"I'm sorry about all of this," Kate repeated. "It's not fair, is it?"

Amy blew out a breath. "We thought everything would be so good. Tim had gotten a great job with the kind of health coverage Jake needed, even though we have to drive farther for treatments. Eventually we wanted to move to Memphis, closer to my parents and my sister, where there's a good cystic fibrosis hospital. We thought we'd found a church where people actually cared about us."

"People do care about you." Kate reached across the table and touched her hand.

"So who went to all the trouble to set up this print shop? If people care about us, why do so many of them refuse to look me in the eye when I'm walking down the street? Even my neighbor has stopped talking to me. She won't let her son play with Jake anymore either." Amy shook her head. "If they have their way, we'll be relocated near a federal prison or living our life without Tim in it at all."

TIM WAS SITTING ON HIS COT, looking weary and defeated, when Kate and Paul went to see him later that same day. At first Kate wondered if he'd been eating, then she realized it was deep, invasive depression that weighed down his shoulders.

"Have you seen Jake?" It was the first question out of his mouth.

"I saw him at lunch," Kate said.

"Is he better? He was coughing so much. I worry about him."

"He's struggling with all of this," Kate said, "but he'll be okay. He's a determined little boy."

Tim got up and started pacing. When he turned his back, Kate saw that his shoulder blades pushed at the fabric of his orange jumpsuit, accentuating his bony form.

"I have to get out of here," he said. "I have to." Then he turned to Kate, shaking his head. "Someone is framing me.

Whoever it is, they know exactly what will put me away for a long time, and they're setting it up. I promise you, I did not rent that storage facility or set up a print shop."

"But they said that your fingerprints were found on some of the items there," Kate mentioned. "Amy even admitted that some of the items could've been yours."

"I can't explain it," he said. "But I promise you, that signature on the lease, it isn't mine."

"We have to prove that," Paul said.

"The authorities should have a list of what they seized to your lawyer either today or tomorrow," Kate said. "There's bound to be something in there that points to someone else, someone other than you."

Tim sat roughly on the lone chair in the cell and raked a hand through his greasy hair.

"Out of curiosity," Kate said, "did you ever hire Bud or Buck Lovelace to work on your computer?"

She'd toyed with the idea ever since she'd learned of the Lovelace's ability in the IT field. Someone knowledgeable would be able to disable the anticounterfeit devices on Tim's scanner and upload the incriminating evidence, given the right opportunity.

"As a matter of fact, I did. A coworker at the bank told me about them. How did you know about that?"

"Conjecture," Kate said.

"Well, I had this virus that kept popping up ads on my screen. I couldn't work at all, and none of my virus software could touch it." He looked from Kate to Paul. "Do you think they could've set me up?"

"How long ago was this?" Paul asked.

"Oh, maybe a month ago, or a little longer."

"It doesn't seem likely," Kate said. "But at least it's something."

Chapter Twenty-Two

Kate turned the car up the winding dirt road to the Lovelace house the next day. The small home was buried in the hills north of Copper Mill. Rusted machinery was littered here and there in the woods like a graveyard for past technology. The yard surrounding the house contained a chicken coop and several outbuildings with tired-looking facades. Chickens pecked at the ground like living lawn ornaments.

Two immense black Labs came bounding out as Kate pulled the car to a stop alongside the largest of the sheds, not sure if she should get out. The dogs barked at her, but their wagging tails belied their true gregarious dispositions.

Climbing out, Kate soothed, "Nice dogs." She patted them on their heads, their long tongues hanging out of their mouths as they tried to lick her hand.

Kate gazed across the lawn. Two new-looking vehicles were parked closer to the house, and a strange sound emanated from the larger shed. She shushed the dogs as she listened to a *ka-chunk ka-chunk* coming from behind the double doors.

A man came out of the house then. At first he looked to be in his forties, but when he came closer, Kate realized it was Bud, Millie's eldest son. He looked distinctly like his father. In his midtwenties, Bud was balding, and his belly hung over his belt as if he were seven months pregnant. He wore thick black-rimmed glasses and squinted when he spoke.

"Dutch! Tillie!" he yelled at the dogs. "Get back."

"They're okay," Kate said, offering a friendly smile despite the trepidation in her gut. She crossed the yard to where he stood. "We've made friends. Haven't we?" She looked at the dogs.

The young man tapped his foot, and Kate realized he was waiting.

Why did her pulse pick up in his presence? She imagined him purposely framing Tim Lourdes, placing clue after clue that would separate the father from the little boy who needed him so.

"What you need Mrs. Hanlon? You lookin' for Ma? She's at work."

Across the yard were two shiny vehicles. The Prowler sat low to the ground, with vintage yet chic lines. The Mercedes was boxy, though equally impressive.

"Can I ask you a few questions, Bud?" Kate asked.

"Uh . . . I'm kind of busy." He thumbed over his shoulder toward the small house, where the porch looked as if it would break loose at any given moment.

"You run a computer business from your home, right?" Kate wasn't about to let the man off quite so easily.

He nodded, interest growing in his eyes. "Is that why you came? You need a computer worked on?"

"And your brother works with you?"

He watched her for a minute before nodding. "He does. It's a good arrangement. Pays the bills, so to speak."

Kate wondered what kind of bills the brothers could have, living with their parents as they did.

She smiled, trying to get a facial expression out of him, but his look went blank. "Listen, like I said, I'm kind of busy right now. I don't have time to shoot the breeze."

At that moment, Kate saw the resemblance between him and his mother.

"I came to ask about Tim Lourdes' computer. You worked on it, right?"

Bud's face darkened, and his brow furrowed above his eyes.

"I heard about what that guy did," he said.

"What he's *accused* of doing," Kate couldn't help but correct him. "He hasn't been convicted of anything."

"Well, the Secret Service has already questioned us, and I know enough about it to know that I don't need to be getting involved in a federal case." He took a step toward her. The dogs took it as a signal because they started growling at Kate.

"I'm not here to cause any trouble," Kate assured. She could still hear that faint sound coming from the faded white shed.

"Like I said, I don't have time for this." Then he said good-bye and made his way back toward the house.

With their master gone, the dogs again became docile,

walking quietly at her side, occasionally giving her hand a lick as she returned to her car. "Thanks a lot," she whispered to the animals.

She figured the noise from that outbuilding held some sort of clue. The shed leaned south. It was missing half its shingles, and the glass was broken out of the four-paned window on the end. The *ka-chunk ka-chunk* grew louder.

Kate studied the building from her spot by her car. There were no other doors that she could see, save the double-wide doors at the front. The windows in the building were too high up to see through. One of the dogs tried to jump up on her, and Kate scolded him to get down. Then she heard footsteps.

Quickly she got into her car and started the engine. She could see the doorknob of the shed's door turning. So she backed up and pulled out of the driveway.

As she made her way down the gravel road, she glanced in the rearview mirror and saw Buck, who watched her departure.

One thought resounded within her. The sound she'd heard, that *ka-chunk ka-chunk*, could easily have been that of a printing press. But then surely the Secret Service agents would have checked it out, wouldn't they? Something wasn't adding up.

KATE HAD BARELY SLEPT. That *ka-chunk* sound had reverberated in her dreams. When Paul came to breakfast the next morning, she must've looked tired, because he said, "What's wrong?" as he bent to kiss her good morning, then took the chair next to her at the oak table.

"Bad dreams." She shook her head. "It's this counterfeiting thing."

He reached for a bag of granola and poured a portion into his bowl, followed by a spoonful of brown sugar.

"I went to see Millie's sons yesterday." She reached for the cereal and helped herself to a bowl, adding milk but no sugar.

Kate had gotten in late the night before, having gone from the Lovelaces' to Pine Ridge to run errands, then to choir practice, so she hadn't had a chance to talk to her husband.

Paul nodded, then ate a spoonful of the granola. "What did you find out?"

"It wasn't so much what I found out as what I heard."

"And that was . . . ?"

"There was a noise coming from one of their sheds. Paul. It sounded kind of like a printing press."

"I don't know, Kate. It's really hard to imagine that Millie could be in on something like that." He set his spoon in his bowl.

"If the Lovelace boys are involved, I can assume that Millie knows nothing about it. But I'm sorry to say that there are more and more clues that suggest her sons might be guilty," Kate went on. "Millie's sons both work from home and are computer experts. They're rarely seen in town. They live in a remote area where it's easy to go undetected. They never go on vacation, then *wham*, they surprise their folks with an expensive trip to Disney World. They buy expensive new cars. They had the opportunity to put incriminating evidence on Tim Lourdes' computer. Buck has a new mystery girlfriend—and a woman's been spotted passing counterfeit bills. Then yesterday I hear the printing-presslike sound coming from one of their sheds."

"Those clues are compelling. But still, everything you just listed is circumstantial. Just be careful, honey. Unless the Secret Service agents find the Lovelace boys' fingerprints on some of those bills, there's no hard evidence." Paul shook his head.

Kate understood his reservations. After all, the Lovelaces were long-standing members of the community. Buck and Bud had graduated from Copper Mill High School, had lived in Copper Mill their whole lives. Millie would be devastated if her sons were involved in illegal activities.

"If they haven't done anything wrong, the evidence will reveal that," Kate assured. "The Secret Service did question them."

"I know." Paul sat back. "But I also know it was Tim Lourdes that they arrested, not Bud and Buck."

THE BRISTOL WAS CLOSED to customers when Kate made her way there the next morning, though the Hamilton Springs Hotel was open as usual for the Fourth of July holiday. Red, white and blue banners hung over the entrance. When Renee had called with the latest rumor—that counterfeits had surfaced at the swank establishment—Kate decided to see if she could find out any more information for herself.

Kitchen staff bustled back and forth, going about their prep work for the coming day. No one seemed to notice her, so she meandered around the building, looking for the sake of looking. It had become part of the job, she supposed, of amateur sleuth. She was merely a concerned citizen who found herself intervening for people in need.

Sybil Hudson, the general manager of the Hamilton Springs Hotel, was bent over her desk when Kate found her in her office. Her glasses were down her nose, and she pushed them up as she stood to greet Kate.

"Kate." Sybil motioned for her to take a seat. "Please, come on in. To what do I owe this honor?"

Kate positioned herself on one of the two wingback chairs across from Sybil.

"I heard that some of the counterfeit bills showed up here," Kate said.

Sybil nodded, her brown eyes intent on Kate. She was an attractive woman who seemed ageless. Her skin was smooth and clear, with faint smile lines at the corners of her eyes. Her brown hair was pulled back in a no-nonsense knot at the nape of her neck.

"We didn't realize it until Monday when the bank called us," she said. "And we've had some others as well."

"What date was that?"

Sybil paused to look at her calendar. "June 30."

"So about a week ago," Kate said as a mental note to herself. She pulled out a pen and a small notebook and wrote the date down. "Whoever prepared your deposit didn't spot the bills?"

Sybil shook her head.

"So if you don't mind telling me . . . what was in Monday's deposit? Just Sunday's earnings?" Kate paused, and when she saw hesitation on Sybil's face, she explained her curiosity.

"The truth is, Sybil, I believe there's more to this case than meets the eye, so I'm trying to do some of my own sleuthing to see if I can come up with anything that's helpful."

"I see. Well, I certainly wish you the best. Let me think . . . I was out of town over the weekend. I usually do Friday's deposit on Saturday morning; then on Monday, we take in the cash from the rest of the weekend. But we kept all three days' earnings in the safe and deposited it in one lump sum first thing Monday morning."

"So last Friday, Saturday and Sunday?" Kate wrote down the dates.

Sybil nodded.

"And was that just the income from the restaurant or both the restaurant and the hotel?"

"Both." She shook her head. "Once we record where the money came from, it's all put together. We keep track of everything on our end, but once it's at the bank, it's all in one account."

"Is there any way I can look at your guest log?"

"I'm sorry, but I can't give that out." She smiled apologetically.

Kate knew she was pushing her luck with the request. "I understand. Let me ask you this: have you ever heard the name Max Lee?"

The woman shook her head. "No, not that I can recall."

Kate chewed her lower lip as she paused to think. "And did the bank tell you what denominations the bills were?"

"Twenties—one hundred and twenty dollars in twenties."

"Was it a busy weekend for the restaurant?"

"Very. We were packed all three nights."

"Did any of your staff mention anything? See anything suspicious?"

"No. It was a pretty standard weekend, I'm afraid. The Secret Service questioned everyone who worked the weekend. No one saw anything."

"Nothing?" Kate asked. "No one seems to know anything."

Chapter Twenty-Three

Old dogs *could* be taught, Kate decided the following Monday. She and Paul were starting to get the hang of dancing. He'd even stopped counting out every step as they memorized their routine. There were still aspects of the dance that needed improvement, like form and style, and dramatic impact. But the fact that they could move from one position to the next without having to concentrate quite so hard meant they were making progress.

The Cline sisters, on the other hand, were naturals. Georgia and Joe Tucker moved across the floor with such ease, it was breathtaking, especially considering Joe's walking stick. Audrey had found a way to work the cane into the routine so it looked like a prop that contributed to the drama of the dance and not like the helpful walking aid that it was.

Evelyn and Fish had definite chemistry on the dance floor—her shy yet admiring demeanor as they moved, and the way he grinned at her as she took his hand were all part of the drama of dance—and it had freed something in the blue-haired twin.

Just when Kate thought she had her figured out, the woman surprised her.

MUCH OF THE REST of that week was spent in dance rehearsals. Paul and Kate would head to the studio just after breakfast, spend an hour on their routine, and then go their separate ways. Kate had come to enjoy the ritual.

She was a morning person anyway, spending time in the Word followed by a leisurely breakfast with her husband, then off to dance. She felt a sense that she was caring for all the essentials in her life before the day really began. It was invigorating. By nine o'clock, she could go about her day, helping whenever Amy Lourdes needed a hand with Jake, visiting Tim in the jail to cheer his spirits or getting some work done in her studio when she wasn't ferreting out more clues to solve Tim's case.

JAKE WAS WRAPPED IN A BLANKET as he sat at the dining room table doing his schoolwork when Kate came over to babysit after dance rehearsal. She set her handbag on the kitchen counter, where Amy was writing a note.

"Keep an eye on him please," Amy said. "He hasn't been quite himself."

"We'll be fine," Kate said, waving her concerns away.

Amy walked over to her son and bent to kiss the top of his head. A burst of coughing rattled his thin frame. She patted his back until it was over. Jake lifted his big eyes.

"Mrs. Hanlon and I will be okay, Mom."

"I know you will."

Once she had gone, Kate took a chair across from the six-year-old. He was so intent on what he was doing that he didn't even lift his head. His eyes scanned the page in front of him.

"Your mom's note says to not let you work too hard," Kate said.

"I like to read," he said.

"What are you reading?"

He turned the book toward her. It was *Curious George* by H. A. Rey.

"I love that book," Kate said. "Can you read it to me?"

His face lit up. They moved to the couch in the living room, and he began to read. Kate could tell that he'd read the book often; it flowed from him as if memorized, but when she pointed out individual words, he knew them immediately.

"You're an excellent reader," Kate said.

"My mom's a good teacher. She says I'm way ahead for my age. But if she has to keep working, she might not be able to teach me like she used to."

"Let's hope your dad will come home soon," Kate said. "Then life can go back to normal."

"But that tall guy said Daddy was *in caboots*. What does that mean?"

"You mean *cahoots*," Kate said. "It means the man thinks your daddy is doing illegal things with a partner. But, honey, you should know that your mommy and I believe that man is wrong."

It pained Kate to know that someone would talk so insensitively to a child. She only hoped she could rectify that injustice. She knew she was getting closer to the truth, little by little. It was a jigsaw puzzle with several key pieces missing, but she would figure it out. She had to.

Another round of coughing overtook the boy. He seemed too weak to defend himself from the onslaught. Kate pounded on his back as she'd seen Amy do. Finally he took a breath in and out, then rested his head on the couch.

"You're getting better at that," he said, though he seemed weaker, more lethargic.

Kate touched his forehead. He was cool.

"Can I have some water?"

She'd already gotten him two glasses of ice water since she'd arrived. "Sure." She got up and refilled his glass.

Jake took a long, slow drink, closing his eyes as the liquid slid down his throat.

"I've been so thirsty," he said. "And tired."

"Do you like chocolate-chip cookies, Jake?"

"Yum," he said, a smile spreading across his face. In that moment, Kate felt glad to see him acting like the child he was.

She moved to the cupboard Amy had shown her before leaving and pulled out the ingredients for her world-famous chocolate-chip cookies.

"I make pretty good cookies," she said. "I'll make you a deal. If you take a good nap while I bake, you can have two warm cookies, okay?"

He nodded compliantly.

Once he'd dozed off, Kate dialed Amy at work. She told her about the thirst and Jake's languid state. "I'm a little worried about him. What do you want me to do?" Kate asked.

"Check him in half an hour and call me." Amy paused. "Thank you, Kate."

Kate hung up. She finished mixing cookie dough—rearranging her mental puzzle pieces about the case over and over—and soon the house smelled of delicious chocolate-chip cookies.

When Kate checked on Jake, he was still asleep, his breathing labored. She watched him for a while, then retrieved a small New Testament from her handbag and read from Romans 12 about what true life in Christ meant.

The first section struck her anew. It read, "Give your bodies to God because of all he has done for you. Let them be a living and holy sacrifice—the kind he will find acceptable." Then later in verse 17, "Never pay back evil with more evil. Do things in such a way that everyone can see you are honorable."

She closed her eyes and prayed fervently for this child and his parents.

"Father, you love the Lourdes family. I know you won't desert them in their time of need. Please don't let false witnesses tear them down. Help them not to return evil for evil but to overcome evil with good. Your Word says that the righteous will prevail, but that seems far from what is happening right now. Please reveal yourself to this family in a miraculous way. I know that you will show your unending love in the big and the small things. And, Lord, I ask you to give me wisdom so I can help them find the truth."

When she opened her eyes, Jake moaned in his sleep. She touched his forehead. He seemed warm, so she slipped a thermometer under his armpit so she wouldn't wake him.

His fever was one hundred and two degrees. She called Amy immediately. "I'll be home right away," Amy said. "He needs to go to Urgent Care."

Chapter Twenty-Four

The Pine Ridge medical staff gathered around Jake practically from the moment Amy and Kate brought him into Urgent Care that Monday. When the nurse had placed an oxygen monitor on his index finger, his levels were dangerously low. She immediately hooked him up to oxygen and started him on an IV. His face flushed, and he no longer seemed to notice when someone came or left the room. Eventually he fell asleep, despite the bright examination room and the uncomfortable-looking vinyl mattress that squeaked with each movement.

"The medicine is helping him sleep," Dr. McLaughlin said when he came in to check on Jake. "And I have him on a strong antibiotic."

"I should really take him to his pulmonologist in Chattanooga—" Amy began, but the doctor cut in.

"If we need to consult him, we sure can. But Jake has to get past whatever is pulling him down right now. If these antibiotics do their job, we might not have to resort to that. But I'm concerned about some of the other things going on with him, quite frankly."

Amy passed Kate a worried look.

"We need to keep his organs functioning properly, and they're struggling right now. There's potential for a lung infection, so with the weakened condition he's in . . . well, let's just say, a little prayer wouldn't hurt." His eyes were kind, caring.

Amy crossed her arms over her chest and studied her son for a long moment. "How long will it be before we know if the antibiotics are doing their job?"

"Shouldn't be too long—next couple of hours. But he will be here at least overnight. Then we can talk about transporting him to Chattanooga, if necessary, sometime tomorrow."

When the physician finally left, Amy lost it. She cried in a blubbering heap while Kate held her. Her thin body shook with each sob.

Finally she pulled back, wiping at the tears that streamed down her cheeks. "I wish Tim was here, you know? This is just wrong. A son needs his daddy at his bedside." She touched the lightweight bedspread that covered him. "They're so close to each other. And Jake has been so brave." Her eyes clouded as she brushed his bangs out of his face. "If I'd been more attentive, maybe he wouldn't have gotten sick."

"Don't say that, Amy. You are an incredible mother," Kate said.

Amy blew out a long breath, still staring at her son. His chest moved up and down in the rhythm of life.

"I'm not nearly as strong as he is."

"You're as strong as you need to be," Kate said.

AS KATE SAT WITH AMY that night and into the next morning, the truth that much of life was beyond a person's control sank in. Jake managed to sleep despite the racking coughs that continued to seize him.

Amy, on the other hand, didn't seem to have slept at all. Kate noticed that she sat by his bed most of the night, sometimes rising to pace the dimly lit room, sometimes simply staring at her son.

At six o'clock, Kate convinced her to go get something to eat, though she protested that she didn't want to miss the doctor when he did his rounds.

"I'll call your cell if he shows up," Kate promised.

Hesitantly Amy obeyed, stopping one last time at the doorway to offer a look at Jake. His eyes remained closed, his face flushed.

As soon as she was alone, Kate pulled out paper and pen from her handbag to see if she could gain a fresh perspective on what she'd discovered in all her sleuthing.

Most of her assumptions about Tim Lourdes' innocence were based on a gut instinct and a few inconsistencies that seemed glaringly obvious to her. Why hadn't the Secret Service agents seen the problem with Tim's supposed motivation for what happened at the church? What possible meaning could there have been, in their opinion, for adding counterfeit money to his own offering?

Sure, there had been the computer evidence and the e-mails to Max Lee. That was compelling, to say the least. And yet with the anticounterfeit devices built in and the printer's dpi limitations, there was plenty of room for reasonable doubt. And, of course, there was the print-shop evidence at the storage facility, where several of Tim's items had been identified along with Tim's fingerprints. But according to Amy and Tim, the signature on the lease wasn't his. Unfortunately, they hadn't heard back from the lawyer regarding the handwriting analysis. What was the holdup on that?

Kate's phone rang. It was Livvy.

"How's Jake? I heard he was admitted," Livvy said.

"Struggling," Kate answered honestly.

"Can you let me know if there's anything I can do? I'll come sit with him, make meals, whatever."

"You could come later today after you finish work," Kate suggested. "Maybe then we can convince Amy to take a nap." She smiled.

"I'll be there," Livvy promised.

Jake coughed as she hung up. How many times had the youngster been in this situation? Battling for life when life should be abundant. His mother was downstairs, buying food at the hospital cafeteria with money she was struggling to earn. Kate wished Amy had taken the offering money. What else was the church for if not to help the hurting?

Maybe that was what God had been communicating to her before, when she'd felt so strongly that he still wanted Kate to help financially. Amy wouldn't take the offering money because it had been given, at least in the eyes of those who would object, under false pretenses.

But if, knowing all they knew now, Amy saw the church responding as Christ would, directly, compassionately, with eyes wide open? Then she couldn't refuse their help, could she? An idea sprung to mind: Kate would host a bake sale, with all proceeds going to Jake's medical expenses.

Dialing again, this time she called her husband.

"You know," Paul said, after she'd told him what was on her heart, "a bake sale might draw out the counterfeiter too."

"I thought of that. But it'd be risky for him."

She'd gone into the hallway to make the call, since it was still early and she didn't want to wake Jake. A nurse walked by, and she lowered her voice. "More than anything, it's an opportunity for the church to show true compassion."

"I'd say that's good enough reason right there."

Kate stared at her phone well after Paul hung up. Perhaps it was unlikely that the counterfeiter would show up at the bake sale, but it wouldn't hurt to be prepared. She'd call around about staffing it with younger Copper Mill folks. Whoever had been passing the bills seemed to prefer inexperienced clerks. And she'd make sure her clerks were on the lookout for the funny money.

JAKE AWOKE BY NOON, though the flush in his cheeks remained, along with the glassy look in his eyes.

"He's not out of the woods," the doctor said as he turned his gaze from son to mother. "He still has a fever, so dehydration is a very real concern. We still need to watch for signs of a lung infection. I'm still debating sending him to T. C. Thompson Children's in Chattanooga, but we'll wait and see for now."

Amy and Jake nodded mutely as if they'd heard those same words time and again.

When Dr. McLaughlin finally ruffled Jake's hair and said farewell, Amy looked at Kate. Kate knew the younger woman was depleted, exhausted from what she'd already endured. She patted her back.

"I'll stay with him. You need to go to work, see your husband."

"I don't expect you to miss out on all your responsibilities though." Amy shook her head. "You have a life to get back to."

Kate shook her head. "I'll be here as long as you need me."

Chapter Twenty-Five

Renee Lambert had come early for that night's regular dance lesson. Kisses whined from his place in the designer bag at her side. She patted his shivering head with her manicured hand.

"I regret not joining in all this excitement," she said to Kate, her eyes on Joe and Georgia as they one-two-three'd across the polished floor before class. Their bodies rose and fell with the beat like horses on a carousel.

"You could do it next year," Kate suggested.

"I suppose, though it won't be nearly the novelty it is this year." She looked at Kate. "Why are you and Paul doing it? You don't really strike me as the type."

Kate wasn't sure what "the type" meant. She chose to ignore the comment. "At first we thought it would be fun, then we realized that if we won, we could help the Lourdeses with the prize money."

Renee huffed and dropped her mouth open. "That perp? Why in the world would you help him?"

"They have a need" was all Kate said, choosing to avoid the open door to gossip.

Renee patted Kisses' head and turned to Evelyn, who had joined them at the side of the mirrored room.

"So," Renee said to her, "what are you planning on doing with the prize money if you and Fish win the dance competition?"

Evelyn pursed her lips as if she didn't want to share the information with Renee, but Renee only leaned closer to her.

"I have plans," Evelyn said evasively.

"You're not going to give it all to that Lourdes family too, are you?" Renee looked accusingly at Kate.

The light in Evelyn's eyes told Kate of her appreciation for the idea, though Kate sensed she wouldn't dare say such a thing in Renee's presence.

"So"—Renee seemed obsessed with digging some sort of information out of Evelyn—"you just love to dance? Is that it?"

"Oh no." She smiled sweetly. "I'm not much of a show person." Her wrinkled face turned up in a smile, and she lightly touched her bluish hair.

PAUL SMILED at the devoted Faith Briar flock the following Sunday. Everyone was in the usual spots. Kate sat near the front, her eyes on her handsome husband. He wore a brown guayabera shirt she'd picked up for him at Belk's. It brought out the blue in his eyes.

"As most of you will recall," he said, "we took an offering several weeks ago for the Lourdes family. Now a lot of talk has been going around town about his arrest and all that followed, and I'm not up here to comment on that. But I do want to talk about a section of Scripture."

Paul bent his head to read. "In Matthew chapter twenty-five it reads, 'Then the King will say to those on his right, "Come, you who are blessed by my Father, inherit the kingdom prepared for you from the creation of the world. For I was hungry, and you fed me. I was thirsty, and you gave me a drink. I was a stranger, and you invited me into your home. I was naked, and you gave me clothing. I was sick, and you cared for me. I was in prison, and you visited me."'"

That Paul had used the same portion of Scripture when they'd taken the offering weeks before seemed a powerful thing to Kate.

Paul went on. "Then these righteous ones will reply, Lord, when did we ever see you hungry and feed you? Or thirsty and give you something to drink? Or a stranger and show you hospitality? Or naked and give you clothing? When did we ever see you sick or in prison and visit you? And the King will say, I tell you the truth, when you did it to one of the least of these my brothers and sisters, you were doing it to me!'"

Paul turned his gaze upon the congregation. "Did you notice the passage didn't say, 'I was wrongly accused and in prison'? or 'I was a stranger, but you had a pretty good idea I wouldn't harm you'? Jesus isn't talking about keeping ourselves safe. This is pretty risky stuff."

He recounted the story of those who did not help the ones who came to their door, those who didn't feed the poor or clothe the naked.

He shook his head. "I have to tell you, I don't think about the needy nearly as often as I should."

As Kate listened, her thoughts turned to Tim Lourdes pacing that jail cell, no visitors aside from his family and his lawyer. And Amy so hurt by her neighbors who wouldn't let their little boy play with Jake.

"And what happened to them?" Paul lifted his face, his expression the picture of gentility, before returning to his text. "And he will answer, I tell you the truth, when you refused to help the least of these my brothers and sisters, you were refusing to help me.'"

He shook his head again. "That's a pretty powerful statement, isn't it? In Texas those are fightin' words!" He chuckled. "It's so easy to get comfortable, to forget. We all do it. Me too." He paused and smiled at Kate. "But this was why Jesus came, to help the down and out, the naked and hungry, the person in prison." His expression was filled with meaning. "He doesn't want us to turn our backs."

There was a hushed silence when he stepped from the podium. No doubt his words had struck a chord with many that day. They had certainly struck a chord with Kate.

The past week, Jake had been transferred to the children's hospital in Chattanooga, making the Lourdes' financial needs even greater, especially because Amy was unable to commute to the dance studio while in Chattanooga. Thankfully, the Harpers had offered her as much time off as she needed.

Kate closed her eyes as the hymn began. Sam Gorman played fervently, pounding out the notes. Even as they left the church, the congregation was subdued, though many stopped to offer their greetings.

Kate looked around to see if the Lovelaces were there. She spotted Millie and Boom, but before she could talk to them, Audrey Harper came up to Kate and Paul, Hal trailing behind.

"Thank you for that message today, Pastor." She reached to shake hands with Paul. "It was very timely." She looked at Hal, who nodded his agreement.

"I'm glad it was meaningful for you," Paul said.

"Like you said, we get so used to having so much. Sometimes we forget, and it can be hard to find opportunities," she said. "Please let us know if there's anything more we can do for the Lourdeses."

"Well," Kate began, "you could donate something to the bake sale for the Lourdeses on Wednesday at the library, if—"

"Say no more!" Audrey held up a pink-manicured hand. "I make a mean peach pie. I'll bring two!"

Chapter Twenty-Six

Dance lessons had just finished that Tuesday night when Audrey called Kate over.

"I totally forgot to bring those pies with me," she said. "But I did make them."

Kate watched her with new eyes. Audrey seemed perfectly fine, though her head bobbed in that nervous way.

"You can bring them by between nine thirty and ten tomorrow," Kate offered, trying to sound normal. They had rescheduled the Wednesday morning rehearsal to the afternoon so they could hold the bake sale in the morning.

"Oh no! I can't make that time. I have a dentist appointment in Pine Ridge."

"No problem. I can stop by your house and get them first thing in the morning," Kate offered.

"Oh, would you?" Audrey looked so thankful that Kate didn't even mind making the trip.

WHEN KATE ARRIVED at the Harper house the next morning, the Lincoln Town Car and Porsche were again parked outside the large garage. Kate pulled up alongside them and got out. She made her way to the front door and had just rung the bell when she noticed a package lying on the front stoop. Bold letters in the upper left-hand corner read "NexTag Comparison Shopping." Kate stared at it.

Audrey came to the door. She had the look of someone in a hurry; her makeup was half done and her hair, which was usually a white halo, was a limp wet rag around her face.

"Come in." She smiled and waved Kate inside. "I'm still getting ready."

Kate stepped across the threshold. "There's a package waiting for you." She pointed out the box.

"Oh, good. I was waiting for that!" She smiled at Kate and added, "Art supplies."

Then she set the box on the narrow table in the entry and bustled to the kitchen, with Kate following behind. She said over her shoulder, "The pies turned out perfect! I added a little extra cinnamon."

Opening her refrigerator, she pulled out each pie, placing them on the granite countertop nearest the fridge. "I put them in these large Ziploc bags. Is that okay?"

"That's great," Kate said. "I really appreciate you doing this."

"It's the least I could do." Audrey paused. "After Paul's message on Sunday . . . well, you know, he was right. We just don't do enough to help others. This is such a small thing to do, and baking is something I enjoy." She smiled sweetly. Then as if remembering the time, she looked at the watch on her wrist. "I've got to fly."

"I can manage these," Kate said, lifting a pie in each hand.

"Let me at least get the doors for you." Audrey went ahead and opened not only the front door but also the front passenger door of Kate's Honda. "I'll probably stop by later to see how it's going," she added as Kate started the car.

She offered a wave and disappeared inside the house as Kate left for the bake sale.

THERE WERE MORE VOLUNTEERS than Kate knew what to do with when she showed up at the library to set up. Four long tables had been placed next to the sidewalk so passersby could happen upon their fund-raiser. Every imaginable baked good was represented—pies and homemade breads, apple crisp, and rhubarb bars, cookies, cakes and donuts. There were so many items that some were piled three deep.

Renee Lambert, with Kisses tucked in the designer bag across her shoulders, ordered around the bake-sale staff with each gesture of her French-manicured fingers, while antiques dealer Eli Weston quietly brought out folding chairs for people to sit on. Several of the young workers stood on the sidewalk holding signs that read "Bake Sale" and "Fund-raiser."

Even Millie Lovelace showed up and hovered near the pies. Kate watched her, feeling guilty for suspecting Millie's sons of counterfeiting. A crowd was gathering as more and more cars pulled into the library parking lot and pedestrians stopped to see what the hubbub was all about.

Renee came up to her, raising a pencil-thin eyebrow. The crowd swirled around them.

"Betty Anderson has a good idea," she said.

Kate glanced at the beautician to whom Renee referred

standing by one of the long tables across the way. A woman whom Kate didn't know came up to Betty and pointed at a bag of cookies. She was tall and had long dark brown hair. Kate started to move toward them.

"Are you listening to me?" Renee insisted, tugging on Kate's arm, pulling her attention with it.

Kate turned her head for just a moment to talk to Renee, but by the time she turned back around, the dark-haired woman had disappeared into the crowd.

"Where did she go?" Kate asked a dumbfounded Betty.

"Who?"

"The woman you just sold cookies to?" She lifted her face to scan the shoppers.

"I didn't see." Betty shrugged.

Kate jogged toward the parking lot, trying to ignore her arthritic knee, then not finding the woman, came back along the sidewalk. The mystery woman was gone.

Kate went immediately to Betty's table, but a line of customers kept her from searching to see if any fake bills had come through. She didn't want to raise a stir, especially given the fact that the fund-raiser itself was for the alleged counterfeiter's family.

Finally there was a lull in the activity, so she pulled the bills out of Betty's cash box and shuffled through them. Nothing. She looked again. She'd been wrong. The woman with the dark hair was nothing more than an innocent bystander.

THE VOLUNTEERS were taking down tables and clearing away leftover baked goods, though there weren't many, as Renee

Lambert tallied up the total sales. The sale had been a huge success. They'd sold almost all of the goods they'd brought. When Kate had called to tell Amy, the young mother had been speechless.

"People *do* care," Kate said.

Amy voiced her thanks, though Kate sensed she was more than grateful for the gesture.

Kate went into the library to thank Livvy for hosting the event. She had just gotten back to the activity outside when Renee jumped up like sliced bread in a toaster. Kisses barked and ran circles around her feet.

"Who took this?" Renee waved a bill in the air. "Who took this?"

Surprised heads turned to see what all the commotion was about.

"What's going on?" Kate asked.

"It's a counterfeit." Renee pushed the bill under Kate's nose.

In the bright sunlight, it was easy to see that the bill was phony—the off-color hue, the slightly fuzzy printing. How had this gotten past them? Kate lifted her head and looked at the other volunteers, who by now had gathered round.

"Which cash box was this in?" she asked.

Renee gave her a blank look. "We combined them."

"The counterfeiter was here?" Justin Jenner, the younger of the two Jenner boys, asked with wide eyes.

Kate held up the bill. "It very well could be."

But no one saw who had passed the money. And other than Kate and Betty, no one else had seen the woman with dark hair.

Who was that dark-haired woman? Was she Buck

Lovelace's girlfriend? Not even Boom and Millie had met their son's love interest, so how could Kate know for sure? She wished she'd gotten a closer look. Betty had been no help. She'd taken the woman's money but hadn't paid close attention to what she looked like.

IT WASN'T UNTIL KATE GOT HOME and was rummaging through her handbag for her checkbook that she noticed the other bill. It was in the middle of her other cash, its fuzzy appearance was undeniable.

Had Renee given it to her with her change when she'd bought bread at the bake sale? Kate studied the bill, knowing she should turn it in to the authorities immediately, but there had to be something here . . . something she could learn by studying the bill.

Carefully, she slipped it back into her purse. Guilt ate at her, yet for Tim Lourdes' sake she would keep it, just a little while. She'd turn it in as soon as she finished examining it.

Chapter Twenty-Seven

The dance competition was less than two weeks away. Kate and Paul kicked practice into high gear, adding a second hour to their daily rehearsal regimen. Since they'd had the bake sale that morning, they'd opted for a late-afternoon session on Wednesday.

"This is still not my thing, Katie," Paul whispered under his breath when he made a misstep, cutting off Kate's path into a spin.

Kate patted his arm and reached up to kiss his cheek. "But it's so sweet of you to hang in there with me."

"Sweet or whupped?" he teased.

"You have the right to back out; I won't hold it against you. For long."

Paul shook his head, then grinned. "A man can't win, can he?"

Kate tucked her face close to his and said in a tender voice, "Honey, you won me thirty years ago." She lightly kissed him, and he pulled her closer.

"You're right about that." He smiled into her eyes and

lifted her right hand, kissing it on the knuckles. "I'm the luckiest man on the planet."

Then they moved back into the Viennese waltz, its enticing rhythm capable of making mature love young again.

"THIS IS BECOMING a regular event!" Audrey said the Friday night when Kate and Paul walked out of their house for another double date with the Harpers. Hal opened the door of his Lincoln Town Car for Kate.

When Kate turned to thank him, she saw the white stain on the cuff of his blue shirt.

Audrey must've seen where Kate's eyes landed because she said, "Honey, you wrecked another shirt!"

Hal's face turned a dark shade of red as he examined the spot.

Audrey wore another flamboyant dress, this one an aqua blue number with rows of ruffles that made up the short skirt. Though the woman wasn't exactly young anymore, Kate suspected that dancing had preserved her figure. A collection of oversized bangles on her wrist made a jangling sound.

Kate and Paul climbed into the backseat of the Town Car, with its plush leather interior and automotive bells and whistles. Soothing instrumental jazz music played through the speakers.

"What is this place we're going to?" Paul asked, leaning forward when he spoke.

"It's a new Italian restaurant in Pine Ridge called the Bologna Café," Audrey said, turning toward them. "It got great reviews in the paper."

She reached into her handbag for the clipping and handed

it to Kate. The article pictured a heavyset man with a beer belly and a wife of equal proportion. Both grinned widely in front of the sign that bore the name.

When she'd finished reading, she handed it back to Audrey.

"We love to eat," Audrey said. "How about you?"

"Are you kidding?" Paul quipped. "You have found your match in us. Kate's a great chef too."

"We'll have to cook together." Audrey turned back to face the front.

Hal had been quiet, which was normal, though he always had that look in his eyes that said he was enjoying the company. Occasionally he'd nod or offer a smile.

"The Cline sisters and I went dress shopping for our costumes," Kate said. "I hope you'll like them."

"Audrey," Paul put in, "I'll be happy if no one breaks a gut laughing while we're onstage."

"It's not that kind of atmosphere, I promise you. Right, honey?" she said to Hal, who nodded. "Everyone is there to support each other. It's about building your confidence so you take the next step in dancing. Besides," she went on, "I think you have a real shot at winning."

Paul chuckled.

"I'm serious!" she protested. She looked at Kate. "Tell him I mean it."

Kate said, "Deep down he believes you."

Paul just grinned.

"How's Amy been with Jake in the hospital?" Audrey asked. "I haven't seen her."

"About as good as can be expected." Kate sighed.

"I know it's hard for her to be away so much right now with Jake in Chattanooga," Audrey said. "I promised her that her job will be waiting when Jake is all better."

Kate watched her as they reached the outskirts of Pine Ridge. Audrey fingered the pearl necklace at her throat.

Chapter Twenty-Eight

Kate and Paul had just settled down to a home-cooked lasagna lunch the next day when a knock sounded on the door. Placing her napkin next to her plate, she went to answer it. It was Audrey Harper.

"I'm sorry I didn't call first," Audrey said, her gray head bobbing. "Is this a bad time?"

"Come on in." Kate motioned her inside.

Audrey held a framed painting in her hands.

"Oh, you're probably eating," she said, glancing at her watch. "I can come back another time."

"Nonsense," Kate said. "Come on in. What do you have there?"

Audrey held up the painting, a watercolor in shades of gray and blue. In it the Smoky Mountains stretched to a faded horizon. The only colors were autumn leaves on the trees in the foreground. It was quite stunning, actually, and Kate paused as she considered it.

"You painted this?" she said.

"Yes . . . I remembered what you said about doing stained

glass, and I thought I'd see if there was any way you could translate this into a window for my pantry door."

She handed the painting to Kate, who led the way to her studio. Paul came from the kitchen and waved to Audrey before returning to his meal.

Kate laid the painting on the light table and turned on the light. "This is lovely." She studied it closer, with an eye to what she would need to do to turn it into a window. "This would be very doable. Do you want to pick out the glass for it?" She pointed to the rack along the far wall with its rainbow of glass choices.

Audrey moved to the rack and oohed over the selection, holding up one piece after the next, searching for the right texture and color to give the effect she was after.

"Is it okay if I take this out of the frame?" Kate said of the painting. "I need to draw up a stencil, and it'd be easier."

"By all means," Audrey said, coming alongside her and turning the frame over. She turned up the clips that held it in place and pulled out the paper.

"Is this regular watercolor paper?" Kate was surprised at its texture. Instead of the heavier watercolor paper she was used to, it was a thin sheet.

"It's rag paper," Audrey said, nodding her head. "I like it because it doesn't curl or get wavy like other papers."

Rag paper. The same paper used to make counterfeit bills.

ONCE AUDREY HAD PICKED OUT her glass choices and approved the quick stencil that Kate drew up, she left for home. Kate then went straight to her computer that lay closed on the kitchen counter. Booting it up, she waited until the machine confirmed that she was connected to the Internet.

Pulling up the Google search page, she typed in the name she'd seen on the package on Audrey's stoop—"NexTag"—along with the word *paper*. Several links popped up, including three that went straight to the NexTag page. Kate clicked on the link. The site was cluttered with listings of their many offerings, from items for babies to gifts and travel to jewelry and watches. The site seemed to sell it all.

"What are you doing?" Paul asked.

"I'm looking up a company on the Internet."

Paul read over her shoulder. "NexTag. What's that?"

"Audrey got art supplies from them. The package was on her doorstep when I went to get the pies for the bake sale."

"And . . . ?" Paul raised a brow.

She shrugged. "I'm following a lead."

She found the search bar for the NexTag site and typed in "rag paper." Sure enough, the company sold the expensive paper. "Look at that price," she showed Paul. It ranged from seventy dollars to almost three hundred dollars for one hundred sheets.

Paul whistled. "At that price, you'd have to print money on it just to afford it."

"I didn't say I suspected the Harpers of counterfeiting." Kate looked at her husband. "They're our friends."

"You wouldn't be looking it up if you didn't."

"YOU WANT TO WHAT?" Livvy said when Kate asked her to come with her the next day.

"I need to see if my suspicions are correct," Kate said.

"Some rag paper, a bleach stain and medicine? That's all you're basing your suspicions on? Audrey said the paper was for her artwork; you've seen her drawings. I don't know about this, Kate. It doesn't seem like very much."

Kate sighed. Livvy made a good point. There was more evidence that Millie's sons were involved. And it felt like a betrayal of their blossoming friendship to suspect Hal and Audrey. After all, of anyone in Copper Mill, they'd been the most giving and open to the Lourdeses, giving Amy a job when no one else would. It would surely be a slap in the face if they found her snooping around.

"You're right," Kate finally admitted. "Would you consider coming with me to Millie's house then? I want to have a talk with her boys, and I could definitely use some moral support."

Chapter Twenty-Nine

Black Labs Dutch and Tillie met Kate's car when she drove up the Lovelace driveway just as they had on her prior visit. Only this time, the dogs didn't bark. They must've recognized Kate, she figured, because they came up with tongues lolling and tails wagging.

Kate and Livvy climbed out of the car and petted the large panting dogs on the head before moving toward the small house. One roofline went one way, the next went another. Kate suspected that the Lovelaces had added on to the house as they had more children, or more money.

She moved ahead to the door, passing several cats that were sunning themselves on the small front porch. Kate knocked, then took a step back as she and Livvy waited for the sound of footsteps. Finally the door creaked open. This was the son Kate had glimpsed at the shed as she'd peeled out of the driveway.

Buck was much thinner than his brother, nice looking in a disguised sort of way, as if all he needed was a good woman to give him a makeover to reveal his charm.

He looked at Kate, and his eyes narrowed.

Kate flinched, then cleared her throat.

"Hi, Buck. Could Livvy and I talk with you for a sec?" she asked.

"What's this about?" He looked from one woman to the other. Then the sound of more footsteps came from behind them.

"Who is it?"

Kate knew the voice was Bud's even before she saw his black-rimmed glasses and his bald head.

"It's the pastor's wife from Faith Briar."

"What does she want now?" He sounded irritated.

Kate exchanged a nervous look with Livvy.

Buck turned and glared at Kate as if sending the question on to her. Kate inhaled deeply, then looked the young man in the eyes. "We just want to ask you some questions."

"Okay . . . ," Bud said.

"I wondered if you'd tell us about your trip to Disney World. Your dad said that you surprised them with the vacation?" She worded it as a question.

Buck crossed his arms over his barrel chest.

"Oh, chill," Bud said to him, leading the way into the house. "Come on in." He waved the women inside.

"Thank you," Kate said. "We won't take a lot of your time."

The living room, while a bit cluttered with magazines and newspapers, had a country feel, with handmade afghans stretched across the backs of the several rocking chairs in the room. The couch, a rust-colored floral print, was encased in clear plastic. Kate and Livvy sat on it.

"So," Kate began, "what made you decide to take the vacation?"

"Ma always wanted to go," Buck said. "Ever since we were little, she talked about going to Disney. She had a thing for that guy in all the *Love Bug* movies. What was his name?"

"Dean Jones," his brother supplied. He was on the rocker farthest from Kate and Livvy, his arms over his chest and a leery expression in his eyes.

"That was really nice of you."

"She does a lot for us." Buck shrugged. "And since our business is doing so well, we finally had the money for it."

"Business? Your IT business?" Kate said. She watched the brothers, looking for any sign that they felt awkward or uncomfortable, but they seemed more shy than anything else.

He nodded. "Some, but mostly it's Geeks in Love."

"Geeks in love?" Kate exchanged a surprised look with Livvy.

"It's an Internet dating site," Buck said.

Bud must've noticed Kate's surprise, because he jumped in. "A lot of people out there are challenged to find a soul mate. The world judges people by how they look, not by their heart. A site like ours allows people to get to know the inside before they judge the outside." He shrugged. "There are a lot of people who are willing to pay for a safe place to meet."

"Do you want to see it?" Buck leaned forward, his brown eyes alight.

"The Web site?" Livvy said.

He nodded, and the women agreed.

Livvy followed behind Kate as they moved down steep stairs into a white concrete block basement. The air smelled musty, and it felt damp, a cold damp. Below was a wide open space that spanned the entire footprint of the house. A

Japanese folded divider created separate "bedrooms" with rumpled, unmade queen-sized beds, dressers and TVs in each. Both sets were on. Stacks of dirty laundry grew like stalagmites from the floor. There wasn't a surface that wasn't cluttered with papers, interspersed with dishes and half-filled glasses of cola that had lost their fizz.

Buck turned left at the bottom of the stairs toward two oversized desks that sat side by side, lit by the blue light of fluorescent bulbs.

"We've connected over three hundred couples already," Buck said proudly as he set up two folding chairs for Kate and Livvy. Bud was booting up the Web site.

"Who knew you were such romantics?" Livvy said as she took her seat and glanced at the screen.

Kate wondered if she was teasing, but the expression on her face said she was completely serious.

Apparently, matchmaking was a thriving business. Page after page of endorsements testified to the accomplishments of the nerdy matchmakers. Buck gave them a virtual tour, starting with a personality-profile test and ending with a photo album of couples who'd tied the knot after finding each other through the site.

"So this is a profitable business?" Livvy asked.

Both brothers nodded. "Our profit is well over a hundred grand already this year," Buck said.

"Wow," Kate said, "that's a chunk of change."

She looked around the room for any sign that the Internet business could be a front for a counterfeiting scheme, but nothing struck her as particularly suspicious. Even the printer was void of paper, and the wastebasket beneath it held scraps, but nothing that looked like counterfeit bills.

Then she noticed that there was a photograph of a woman taped to the upper left-hand corner of the computer. She was blonde, with pale blue eyes.

"Who's the pretty girl?" Kate motioned to the picture.

Buck's eyes followed. He grinned. "Natasha," he breathed. "She's my girlfriend. I met her through the site. She lives in Delaware."

Natasha was no dark-haired mystery woman. And she lived in Delaware? Confusion swept through Kate. If she wasn't the woman passing counterfeit bills, who was?

"So"—Kate sat back—"can I ask you something else?"

"Sure," Buck said, turning to look at her.

"What's in the shed out front?"

Chapter Thirty

Buck pulled a key chain from his pocket and fit a key into the ancient lock, then opened the door, revealing the dark interior. Dust motes floated in the air above, where the transom windows let in what light there was. He flicked on a lone lightbulb that swung overhead. A large antique machine took up the center of the room. Kate had no idea what it was, though she knew it wasn't a printing press. They walked around it.

"It's a threshing machine," Buck answered. "It was built in 1889. The real deal. I got it up and running again. It sat in a farmer's shed for a good thirty years."

"What are you going to do with it?" Livvy said, lightly touching the metal wheel on the side.

"Take it to threshing shows," Bud said from the other side. "In July we showed it at the thresherman's show in Madison, Kentucky. That's where he finally met his new girlfriend."

"Face-to-face?" Kate turned to Buck.

Buck turned a bright red. "She's into threshing shows too."

AS THEY DROVE HOME, Kate rolled through her mental list of evidence while Livvy spoke briefly with her husband on her cell phone. So many clues had led to the Lovelaces' door, and yet she'd been wrong. Two men, a woman. Their seeming sudden wealth.

Wait. A thought came to her. Hadn't Agent Wimper said that the counterfeit bills were all pre-1996? What was significant about that year?

She turned to Livvy as her friend tucked her phone into her handbag. "Can you do me a favor?"

Livvy glanced across the seat at her. "Anything," she said.

"Can you find out what happened in the printing of money between 1996 and 1997?"

"Okay. And why is this significant?"

"Do you remember the town meeting with Agent Wimper?"

Livvy nodded.

"He said all the counterfeit bills were pre-1996."

Kate saw the lightbulb go on.

"I'll look into it right away."

"Thanks, Watson."

Livvy winked. "Gotcha, Sherlock."

KATE STOPPED BY THE LIBRARY shortly after lunch on Monday.

"Okay, I found out some stuff you're going to like," Livvy began as they each took a seat in Livvy's office. Excitement beamed from Livvy's eyes.

She laid some printouts between them. "I got this information from moneyfactory.gov. It talks specifically about the changes that happened in 1996."

"Yeah?"

"It seems that in 1996, the government decided to buckle down on counterfeiting. So they introduced several new features to the currency that are much harder for the layperson to reproduce." She pointed to a highlighted section of the text and went on. "The new features found in the Series 1996 $20, $50 and $100 notes, and the 1999 Series $5 and $10 notes—including an enlarged off-center portrait, watermark, fine-line printing patterns and color-shifting ink . . ."

"That's why he's duplicating older bills," Kate deduced. "They're still legal tender, and they're easier to fake." She sat back. "This person knows a lot about what he's doing." Her eyes met Livvy's.

Kate reached into her bag and showed Livvy the bill from the bake sale. She was relieved to share the secret with her friend.

"This was in my handbag after the bake sale."

Her heart pounded in her chest as she laid the note in front of Livvy who pulled out a magnifying glass from one of the drawers in her desk behind them. She turned on the light over the table. "What do you see?" Kate said.

Livvy bent to study the bill, moving the magnifier from place to place. "Do you have a real one?" she said, lifting her gaze.

Kate pulled a genuine twenty from her handbag and set that alongside the phony.

After a few more minutes, Livvy pushed the money back to Kate.

"The real money is much more intricate and detailed"—

Livvy paused—"though there were parts of the fake that seemed pretty refined too."

"I saw the same thing," Kate confirmed. "There are sections on the bill, particularly near places that denote its denomination, that are faded."

"I didn't catch that." Livvy sat back. "What does that mean?"

Kate reached for the counterfeit again and found the spot she'd located earlier. She pointed for Livvy to have a look. "Do you see the security thread along the side?"

Livvy bent again to search for it.

"One thing our counterfeiter forgot"—Kate spoke while Livvy examined the bill—"is that pre-1996 money still had the security threads. Where it should say '$20' in fine, fine printing, this one says '$5.'"

A grin spread across Livvy's face. "So what does that mean?"

"This isn't fake money," Kate said. "It's one hundred percent real. At least it started out that way. The counterfeiter is bleaching sections of lower-value bills and reprinting them in larger denominations. That's why the serial numbers are authentic; that's why the bills feel like real money; that's why the counterfeit checking pens don't work on them."

"That's genius! But not all the bills have been done this way, right? The pens have caught some of the money . . ."

"Exactly. Do you remember that Agent Wimper said the bills were manufactured in different ways? I think this is what he meant. Some are totally fabricated, and some are like these—real bills bleached and reprinted."

Livvy was shaking her head.

"There's one surefire way to test it," Kate said.

Kate took Livvy to the library's soda machine.

"Isn't this illegal?" Livvy said. "You're trying to pass a counterfeit bill."

"I can pay the library back in real money if it spits out a can."

Livvy's shoulders relaxed. She took a deep breath at the same time Kate did. Kate pulled the twenty-dollar bill out of her billfold and flattened it out before lifting it to the machine's cash slot. The bill slid inside easily before being burped back out. Kate's eyes met Livvy's, then she flattened the bill a bit more and tried again. This time it went in, followed by the sound of quarters piling into the change dispenser. Kate bent to pull out three dollars and seventy-five cents in change.

The machine thought she'd put in a five-dollar bill.

KATE AND LIVVY went immediately to the deputy's office, where they found Skip reading the previous week's *Chronicle*.

"What can I do for you ladies?" He quickly removed his feet from the desktop, where they'd been resting. "Did you want to visit Tim?" He started to stand to get the cell's keys. "He sure has had a lot of visitors today."

"We're looking for Agent Norris," Kate said.

The deputy sat back in his chair. "That right? Or maybe I can help you . . ."

Kate noted how he puffed out his chest ever so slightly.

"No. We really need Agent Norris. Sorry, Skip," Kate said.

"That's okay, Mrs. Hanlon. I guess Norris is probably at his hotel room."

IT SEEMED THE US GOVERNMENT had cash to spare when it came to housing their Secret Service agents on special missions. Kate and Livvy found Agent Norris at the Hamilton Springs Hotel. Kate had called his cell number, which she got from the business card he had distributed, telling him that she had new information in the case. He invited her and Livvy up to talk.

It struck her as a bit odd, being invited into the man's hotel room, especially considering his earlier rebuff for her sleuthing on the case. But there was much about the man that struck Kate as odd, and she felt glad that Livvy was by her side.

"You say you have new information?" He met them at the door, his tall frame looming, his eyes penetrating.

"We do." Kate nodded, her heart pounding in her chest.

He opened the door wider, allowing them to come inside. The room was immaculate, not even a wrinkle on the beds. The TV remote lay on top of a glass-topped table.

Agent Norris led them to the seating area, where Kate and Livvy took the couch like nervous teenagers at a job interview. Why should she feel nervous? Kate wondered. But there was something different about that afternoon's encounter. Something about the way the man held himself. No doubt it was his large-and-in-charge attitude. She took a deep breath and smiled at him, glancing down at his loafers.

Kate laid the counterfeit bill Livvy had retrieved from the soda machine on the table.

The blond agent raised an eyebrow.

"It was one of the fake bills from the bake sale," Kate explained, her face turning red with the admission.

His brow puckered.

Kate cleared her throat and went on. "I must've gotten it in change. When I examined it more closely, I noticed that it has faded areas."

The agent nodded as if he was already aware of the fact.

"If you'll look closely, you'll see that the security thread, that should read '$20,' in fact reads '$5.'"

The man's face blanched. He glanced at the note. "Really?" He seemed surprised. Even a bit offended.

Kate hated one-upping the man, but he should at least have been grateful that she was sharing information with him. Shouldn't he? Agent Norris got up abruptly and shuffled through a box on the floor on the opposite side of the room. He returned with a magnifying glass and bent to study the note.

When he lifted his face, Kate could tell he'd figured out the implications of the discovery too.

"You see," Kate said. "It's *real* money. This person is bleaching the denomination sections on lower-value bills and reprinting them at a higher value." She paused to allow the man to take in the meaning of her words.

Finally Agent Norris met her eyes. "You're a pretty smart woman, Mrs. Hanlon." He shook his head. "Have you told anyone else this?"

"No, just you. And Livvy here, of course."

Livvy offered a meek smile.

"Well, I appreciate you letting me know."

"But don't you see?" Kate went on. "It means that Tim Lourdes can't be guilty."

The agent scratched his head, and his thick brows knit together over his crooked nose. "How did you come to that conclusion?"

"There was no bleach found at the storage facility, no sink to rinse it or water and soap to neutralize it."

The agent shook his head. "All that means is he bleached it somewhere else and did only a portion of the work there." He pursed his lips. "It makes sense from a criminal perspective to use multiple sites—less evidence all together."

Kate's heart sank.

"I'm going to take this into evidence, if that's okay with you," Agent Norris said, pointing to the bill.

"Of course."

"And . . . uh . . . thank you again, Mrs. Hanlon. You've shed some light on a lot of things today."

Chapter Thirty-One

That night, Jake Lourdes took a turn for the worse. Kate rushed to the hospital in Chattanooga when Amy called with the news.

When she walked into the ICU waiting room, Amy informed her, "His lungs are infected. It's a bad one this time."

THE NEXT FEW DAYS were torture for the Lourdes family. Kate had seen it in the listless way Amy looked at her. The young woman was losing heart.

Not only did Jake make no progress physically, it seemed the courts had stalled with regard to moving up Tim's trial. Tim's lawyer had made a motion to that effect shortly after Jake was transferred to Chattanooga, yet, given the gravity and nature of the crime he was alleged to have committed, the judge wouldn't budge. Due process, he'd asserted, meant that all parties would have enough time to prepare for the upcoming trial.

When the option of bail came up, the judge asserted that anyone capable of avoiding the law as long as Tim had could just as easily slip into oblivion and never be heard from again.

Yet every time Kate went in to see Tim at the jail, his spirits seemed lifted, his hope renewed even though circumstances had become more difficult. No doubt the many visitors who now came to see him—as a result of Paul's sermon, no doubt—did much to bolster his faith. And, Tim had said, he'd been reading the letters of the Apostle Paul.

"I understand what it means to be falsely accused," Tim said to Kate on Wednesday, "and to be powerless to defend myself. Having everyone thinking I'm a thief and a liar." He shook his head and blew out a breath. "I've come to realize that's how it was for Christ. Even though he could've said, 'Hey, they're lying about me! Don't you know who I am?' he just took it. Do you know how hard that is? To have someone think something bad about you and not say a thing to defend yourself?"

Kate nodded as a smile grew on her lips.

"Yet," he went on, "it doesn't matter to me anymore—what people think. They can think I'm guilty, but I know that God sees my heart, and he loves me as I am." He leaned forward, a light in his blue eyes. "That's so powerful—to be able to lay my full self out there and still be accepted."

"That's what forgiveness is," Kate said.

"I never understood it on this level before." Tim laughed to himself. "Who knew that jail could be a good thing in some ways?"

"God works all things—" she began, paraphrasing the Scripture, but Tim finished it.

"To the good for them that love God and are called according to his purpose."

"He does," Kate confirmed. "And he will for you and your family."

IT WAS A GOOD THING Tim was feeling renewed in his faith, Kate realized the next morning when Amy called.

"What's wrong?" Kate asked.

"Jake's lung collapsed last night."

Kate's heart hammered with the news. "Is he okay?"

"He's stable, but they're saying he needs a lung transplant."

"Oh, Amy. I'm so sorry." Kate was devastated. She closed her eyes.

"I don't know what to do, Kate." The panic in her voice sent a pang through Kate's heart.

"What's Jake doing right now?"

"Sleeping."

"Have you gotten any rest yourself?"

"How can I?" Amy began.

"You'll get sick if you don't take care of yourself, Amy. Then what good will you be to Jake?"

"I'll lay down when I get off the phone," she promised.

Kate put a smile in her tone. "I'll come as soon as we get off the phone, okay? You can take a break, maybe even drive home and spend a little time with your husband. He misses you."

"I miss him too." Amy's voice cracked.

"Then it's settled." Kate looked at her watch. It was seven o'clock. "I have to gather a few items and leave a note for Paul. I'll be there as soon as I can."

KATE WATCHED the six-year-old boy as he slept. He reminded her of her own son, Andrew, at the same age—that sweet innocence, especially in slumber, the way his hair spiked in every direction and his long lashes kissed his cheeks. He moaned and moved his head from side to side. Kate touched his hot brow. How long had he had that fever? Almost involuntarily, a prayer rose in her for the little boy.

When she lifted her head, he was looking at her. His face was flushed, and his eyes lacked their usual luster.

"Where's my mom?" he said, casting his eyes around the room.

"I told her to go home, to sleep. She's really tired."

Jake nodded his understanding.

"How are you feeling?" Kate brushed his bangs from his forehead.

"Thirsty."

Kate retrieved the plastic water pitcher and filled it with cold water before returning and pouring water into the cup on his tray. Then she pushed the button that changed the bed's position so he was sitting up. Jake took a slow drink.

"I had a dream," he finally said when he set the cup back on the rolling table.

Kate returned to the chair next to his bed.

"We were all together," he went on. "Me, Mommy, Daddy. And there was that man." His brow puckered, forming a line above his nose.

"What man?"

"That one who said Dad was in cahoots."

"Agent Norris?"

"He was looking at me, and I was asleep again."

Kate stared at the boy as a memory flashed. The night she'd gone to the Lourdes' home after Tim's arrest, Jake had been at the neighbor's. Had he seen the man before she arrived? She didn't think so.

"Jake," Kate said. "Did you talk to Agent Norris the night your daddy was taken to jail?"

Jake shook his head. "*Nuh-uh.* I didn't see him that day. He came the next morning. Mommy was outside, talking to the neighbor."

"Did she let him in the house?"

"Nope. He told me to be very quiet, that he didn't want me to get her."

Kate frowned. "Did he say why?"

Jake's eyes clouded, and he stared at the blanket.

"Jake," Kate prompted. She touched his hand where it rested on the bed. "It's okay. You can tell me."

"He said Daddy was a bad man, in cahoots. Then he said he had to get more evi . . . stuff to prove to the judge what Daddy had been doing."

Kate stared at him. "Did you see what he took?"

"All kinds of stuff. He had a box of things that were laying around the house."

"Are you sure?" Kate leaned forward.

"Yup."

AS SOON AS JAKE FELL ASLEEP, Kate called Lincoln Finch. He answered on the fourth ring.

"Do you have the list of evidence found at the storage facility?" she said.

"It's here somewhere," he said. She could hear him rummaging through paperwork. Finally his deep voice came back on the line. "It's a long list. Do you want me to read it to you over the phone?"

"Can you fax it to the hospital?"

"Sure. I think I have the number here somewhere. Are you looking for something in particular?"

"Jake told me that Agent Norris came by the house after they'd confiscated Tim's computer and office equipment. He told Jake not to tell anyone."

There was silence on the line. "So what did he do while he was there?"

"Apparently, he found some more evidence," Kate said.

"That's not so unusual."

"Telling a little boy not to tell his mother?"

"I meant coming back for additional evidence. So what do you think it was that he took?"

"I'm hoping the list will help me figure that out."

The document was there within a half hour of her call.

Kate gave a quick glance at Jake, who had fallen back asleep, as she took it from the attendant who brought it to Jake's room.

She studied the pages, looking for anything significant. Anything to prove that the print shop at the storage facility had been a setup. Then she saw it. And what she saw surprised her.

Chapter Thirty-Two

Kate called the lawyer back immediately.

"They're sure it was this brand and model?" Lincoln Finch asked.

"I lost a camera that night, *after* Tim was arrested. It was the same model and brand."

"That doesn't mean it's the same one."

But Kate knew it was the same. There was no other explanation. The lawyer shuffled through his copy of the paperwork. "I don't think they've examined that piece of evidence yet. At least I haven't gotten any of the findings."

"Is there any way I can look at the camera, see if it has my photos on it?"

"Doubtful. It's already at the lab."

"Whoever took it from the Lourdes' set Tim up," Kate said. "Don't you see? They didn't know it wasn't Tim's when they planted it at the storage facility. I had never been to their home before that night."

"You're saying Agent Norris set him up?"

"I'm saying that whoever took it set him up. If it was Agent Norris, then yes. And there's something else." She paused, then said, "Agent Norris was wearing loafers without socks the other day."

"So?"

"Abby Pippins saw a stranger at the church the Sunday of the offering."

"Let me guess," the lawyer said. "He wore loafers without socks." There was a long silence on the line before the attorney said, "I'll see about getting that camera examined right away."

KATE CALLED LIVVY shortly after talking with the lawyer.

"Amy's not back yet," Kate informed her. She moved into the hallway so Jake wouldn't be awakened and told Livvy about the new evidence.

"You think Agent Norris is involved?"

"Somehow, though I don't have it all worked out yet. When the evidence comes back on the camera, we'll have something concrete."

"And the Harpers?" Livvy asked.

Audrey had done so much for Amy and Tim, and yet what if that had merely been a ruse? A way to make her look innocent or to assuage her guilt?

The image of Hal talking to Agent Norris at the VFW in Pine Ridge stuck with her. There had never been any mention of counterfeit bills showing up at the studio. So what had the two talked about? Kate already had her suspicions.

THE COUNTRYSIDE PASSED in a blur, blue-ridged mountains occasionally coming into view beyond the towering trees that lined the road. Amy had returned to Jake's room at noon, claiming that sleep was an impossibility, so she might as well stay at her son's side.

Kate couldn't blame her. She would have done the same given the circumstances. So she left around two o'clock for Copper Mill.

It had been all she could do not to blurt out the new discoveries to Amy. But Kate knew the young mother had enough on her plate without the added stress. Once Kate had unraveled the whole web of clues and freed Tim, then she could explain everything.

When she came to the turnoff for the Harpers' estate, Kate took it.

The Porsche was parked in front of the three-car garage as it usually was, but the Town Car was nowhere to be seen.

Kate took note of the expensive car parked outside. It seemed odd considering that they had a perfectly good three-car garage. True, there were a lot of people with cluttered garages, but Hal and Audrey's house was immaculate.

Kate pulled the Honda around the back side of the structure, where it wouldn't be visible to anyone just pulling up. There was a service road on that side of the house, a set of tracks through the woods, but it would make for a good exit route should Kate need it. Kate pulled the car onto the path, a good twenty yards into the trees, before killing the engine and unbuckling her seat belt.

"Let's have a look around," she whispered to herself.

She was careful to shut the car door without a sound, save for a click that said the latch was secured. Then she moved stealthily toward the home. All was quiet. The only sound was that of the breeze in the trees and the flagpole line in front flapping against metal. Kate could hear the distant sound of trucks on the highway below.

She moved to the back of the garage when the sound of a car door slamming met her ears.

Quickly she looked through the back window into the garage. She could see just enough to get a better view. There was some sort of machinery against the far wall. She could see the lower section of it though the rest was covered by a white sheet.

Voices floated toward her from the front of the house. She quickly scanned the room. She could see a sink in the corner and two large bottles marked "bleach" in bold lettering, as well as quart-sized cans that looked like paint.

She knew she had to get out of there.

She ran toward the woods, her heart pounding in her chest as much from the adrenaline rush as from the physical exertion. She heard her knees crack as she ran, a painful reminder of the osteoarthritis she suffered. But escape was a must—pain or no pain.

The edge of the woods was lined with thick lilac bushes. So Kate ducked behind them, casting glances toward the house as she made her way to the car. No one seemed to have heard her. At least no one followed her outside.

She'd seen the bleach bottles and the machine that could easily have been a printing press. Kate started the car, thankful that it had a quiet motor.

It was all starting to add up. The Texas accent. The rag paper, the constant flow of money.

Kate dialed Livvy to tell her what had happened.

"Doesn't it strike you as odd," Kate said after she'd told her about the machine in the garage along with the jugs of bleach and ink, "that they chose Copper Mill as the town to move to even though they had no ties here? They know no one in town . . ."

"Wow," Livvy said, awe in her voice. "What are you going to do?"

"That's what I need to figure out."

Chapter Thirty-Three

For the next couple of days at dance rehearsals, Kate watched Hal and Audrey for any slipups, any sign that her suspicions were true. She thought about telling the sheriff of the odd-looking machine, but she wanted to be sure before she went accusing the quiet dance instructor.

She'd heard through the grapevine that the two Secret Service agents had left town, awaiting the findings from the print shop at the storage facility. When she'd called Lincoln Finch about the camera, he'd said something was holding up the findings, though the specifics were sketchy.

THE NIGHT OF THE dance competition finally arrived. Kate was full of nerves on more than one account. If only she'd had time to pull that sheet back and see for herself what Hal housed in his garage that was so precious he couldn't park his Porsche in there.

The Pine Ridge Country Club, where the competition was being held, was full of practicing, nervous couples. Many were much younger than Kate and Paul. There were even children and early teens, though thankfully they competed in different categories. Kate could just see her and Paul being outdone by a gap-toothed six-year-old couple.

She bent to look in the mirror one last time before it was her and Paul's turn to take the floor, but a large woman blocked her view. Paul stood to the side, just off the performers' entrance to the dance floor, tugging on his tuxedo sleeves, which were an inch too short. He'd had the thing fitted twice, and still it wasn't right.

Finally the large woman with big hair moved out from in front of her, and Kate caught sight of herself. She barely recognized herself. Her dress was form fitting and covered in sequins from neckline to floor. She shimmered like wet nail polish when she moved, and her makeup had the dramatic overexaggeration that was essential in ballroom dance competitions. Thick eyeliner and bright shadow made Kate feel more like a raccoon than a dancer. She lightly touched her hair, which was a helmet of hair spray. Taking a deep breath, she made her way to Paul and the Cline sisters who'd joined him.

The audience applauded as the couple before them in the lineup pranced off the dance floor.

"Where is he?" Evelyn looked frantic. She was dressed to compete, in feathers and fringe.

"Fish?" Kate asked.

Evelyn nodded. "I think he's standing me up!" She inhaled.

Kate could see the tears that shimmered in her eyes.

"I knew this was a bad idea!" She put her face into her hands.

Georgia patted her back and tsk-tsked. Her blue hair was particularly high in a sort of Martha Washington do. The dress she wore carried on the late 1700s theme, complete with a wide bustle and petticoats.

"Don't worry, dear," Georgia comforted. "He'll be here." She said the words, but her expression clearly communicated a disdainful *Men! You can't trust 'em!*

Evelyn lifted doubtful eyes. "You think he'll come?"

Georgia looked compassionately at her sister. "Why don't we go take our seats and cheer for Kate and Paul, eh?"

Evelyn turned to the Hanlons, finally nodding as she wiped the tears from her made-up face.

"She'll be okay," Georgia whispered to Kate before they left. "I can't say the same for Fish when I get done with him."

Kate smiled at their retreating backs before she turned to Paul. "Ready?" she said.

"As I'll ever be." Paul's face held a hint of a smirk, and Kate wondered for a moment whether he was secretly enjoying this.

The announcer's voice boomed over the speakers. "And next in the American-style Smooth Dance competition, from Copper Mill, we have the pastor-and-wife team of Paul and Katherine Hanlon performing the Viennese waltz."

Kate and Paul moved into position, heads lifted, backs slightly arched. Silence. Then the music began, a Johann Strauss piece that Audrey had chosen.

Kate caught sight of Audrey watching from the front row, her gaze intent upon them. She offered a bright smile that Kate awkwardly returned as they moved into the next turn.

Doubt pulled at Kate. How could she suspect a couple who'd been nothing but kind and generous of such an awful crime—not only the counterfeiting but framing Tim and separating him from the family who needed him so desperately?

Then she realized, as Paul led her in the routine, that she didn't see Hal. She glanced over Paul's shoulder as they moved across the floor. Then she saw him standing near the exit sign talking to someone. Paul's head obstructed her view for a moment. When she got a clear view, she saw it was Agent Norris. They were huddled in close conversation, and certainty filled Kate. Perhaps Audrey was sweet and likable, but those two men weren't casual acquaintances. They were business partners.

Paul tripped then, catching the hem of Kate's dress. It wouldn't have been too noticeable except for the tearing sound that accompanied it. Sequins scattered across the polished floor. The hem tangled around Kate's high-heeled shoe, and in a slow-motion moment, Kate and Paul fell. It was a graceful moment, but then it was gone, eclipsed by the tangle of limbs and gasps from the crowd.

The music kept right on while they lay there. Paul exchanged a look with Kate, and then they started laughing. He lifted her to a standing position, but with the torn state of her dress, Kate knew their dance had just ended. Paul bent down and tore what his shoe had started, turning the floor-length dress into an above-the-ankles number. The audience erupted into applause and friendly laughter. Kate grinned and waved at the crowd before she and Paul took a bow.

Then, with shoulders back and heads raised, they walked off the stage hand in hand, where they broke into fits of laughter.

"Promise me you won't make me go back out there," Paul begged Kate.

"I don't know. We did pretty well, didn't we? Right up until you knocked the wind out of me."

"I don't know what you two are laughing about," Georgia said when she returned backstage. "That was horrible. They had to sweep the dance floor because of all the sequins you spilled!"

Kate wiped tears from her eyes, she was laughing so hard.

Joe Tucker came up from behind Georgia.

"That's going to be a hard routine to beat from a crowd-pleasing standpoint," he said, a glint in his eyes.

The announcer's voice came over the speakers as the dancers who'd followed Kate and Paul finished their turn.

Georgia took a deep breath. "We're up soon."

Joe looked relaxed, calm enough to take a nap.

"I'd better get changed," Kate said to Georgia, motioning toward the dressing room. "I want to watch you dance, but there's no way I'm going out there again in this getup."

"Evelyn and Audrey are saving seats," Georgia said.

Kate hurried to get changed while Paul went to sit with everyone else. She wiped the thick makeup from her face and slipped on a knee-length dress in a pale shade of pink just as the announcer gave the cue for Joe and Georgia to take the floor. She glanced around, trying to get another look at Hal and Agent Norris, but they'd left. Evelyn seemed calmer, though she wrung her hands together until her knuckles turned white.

A hush fell over the crowd. Kate's nerves tingled in anticipation of her friends' dance. Evelyn was biting her lower lip. Kate lightly touched her shoulder, and the aged bank teller smiled.

"He'll come," Kate said.

Evelyn shook her head. "He called, Kate. Something came

up." She shrugged. "But that's okay. Georgia can have her moment of glory."

Her smile was tremulous, and Kate sensed she was trying to be brave.

Evelyn went on. "I get so nervous for her." Her eyes crinkled into a smile, then her gaze returned to the dance floor. The music started with a much slower beat than Kate and Paul's had been.

Joe was definitely a leading man. He moved Georgia across the floor effortlessly despite the walking stick. Georgia look like a spinning doll in a jewelry box, if such spinning dolls wore bustles. Audrey seemed mesmerized by their movement.

She must've felt Kate's scrutiny because she shifted in her chair before looking back to the dance.

Kate felt like a traitor.

Soon the music faded, and Joe and Georgia took their final pose. They had done a superb job. The crowd erupted in deafening applause. They waved and moved to the chairs where they would await their scores.

"How do you think they'll do?" Kate heard Evelyn whisper to Audrey.

"Well," Audrey said, "they're at the top of the competition. They'll definitely make finals."

Soon the scores were announced. Audrey's prediction had proved dead-on.

"Let's congratulate them," Audrey whispered to Kate and Evelyn.

So at the next break in the show, the women left in search of Joe and Georgia.

"That was amazing!" Evelyn cooed over her sister as she reached for a hug.

Kate patted her on the back. Joe just grinned. He didn't need to say a word.

"Is it hot in here?" Georgia stepped back from Evelyn and fanned herself. "I'm so hot." Then her eyes rolled back in her head. In an instant, she was on the floor, unconscious.

Kate knelt down and turned Georgia onto her back, then put her ear near her mouth.

"She's breathing," she said. Then she checked her pulse and nodded. "She has a pulse."

"Georgia, honey." Evelyn was at her head, patting her cheeks as she spoke. Her voice was weak with obvious fear. "Wake up, Georgia. Wake up."

The elder sister's eyelids fluttered, and she waved her hand in front of her face as if trying to shoo a fly. "Would you stop that? It's so annoying."

Kate inhaled relief.

"You're okay," Evelyn said.

"What happened?" Georgia pulled herself to a seated position.

"You just made the finals," Kate informed, "then you passed out."

Georgia touched her forehead as she closed her eyes. "I don't feel so good."

"Did you eat anything today?" Evelyn bent next to her in motherly fashion.

"Yeah. I had a banana."

"That's all?"

Georgia shot her a look that clearly said, *Back off!* "Good night, Evelyn, I'll be fine. Stop being so clucky."

The expression on the younger twin's face said she was wounded by the reprimand, but she straightened and gave Kate a weak smile.

"Now," Georgia said, "can someone help me up?"

She looked at Joe, who offered her a hand. But as soon as she was on her feet again, the same pale look came over her. Only this time, Joe caught her and helped her to sit.

"You need to see a doctor," Kate said.

"I need no such thing." Her head was between her hands when she spoke. "We just made the finals—are you insane? Joe and I are going to win that prize money, and that's all there is to it." She sighed and closed her eyes. "Just give me a few minutes."

Then Audrey said to Georgia, "We'll go get you something to drink, okay?"

Georgia nodded without saying a word.

"She wasn't trying to be rude," Audrey said to Kate as they rushed into the hallway.

"I know," Kate said. "She's put a lot into this."

They reached the Coke machine, and Audrey pulled a crisp five-dollar bill from her handbag, slipping it into the bill slot. The machine took it at first, then spit it out.

"That's odd," Audrey murmured. Quickly she stuffed the money back into her wallet, riffling through it for another bill.

"What's wrong?" Kate played innocent.

"Do you have something smaller?"

"I left my handbag with Georgia and Evelyn."

"The machine doesn't want to take my money." She looked around as if trying to think fast.

"We could head to concessions," Kate offered.

Audrey's eyes lit up. "Perfect."

She led the way and gave the five to the teenager at the booth, who looked to be too young to even have a job. He handed her the large soda and her change, and Audrey started back toward Georgia and the others.

When she was just out of earshot, Kate caught the young man's attention and said, "Would you do me a favor and put that bill aside? I'll be back in a few minutes."

He gave her a puzzled look but did as she'd asked. Kate quickly caught up to Audrey, who'd seemed preoccupied with returning to her student.

Georgia looked no better when they returned. She reached for the Coke and drank deeply.

"Would y'all stop hovering over me?" she scolded. "I said I'll be fine."

"We don't have to do this." Joe leaned over to talk to her.

Georgia glared at him. "You want to back out on me now?"

Joe held up his hands. "I never said that."

"Good."

The announcer's voice came over the loudspeaker. "Will the finalists in the American Smooth Dance competition check in with the judges, please? We'll be starting that round in just a little bit."

"That's us," Georgia rose. She placed the flat of her hand on her chest. "Y'all go take your seats. You don't want to miss this."

"Let me fix your hair," Evelyn said, touching the blue mass that had collapsed when her sister had.

Georgia turned to look in one of the many mirrors sprinkled throughout the backstage area. "All right," she conceded.

Kate and Audrey made their way toward the exit and back down the hall to the competition.

"I'm going to stop in at the ladies' room," Kate said. "Can you save my seat?"

"Of course," Audrey said. She pushed through the exit and was gone.

Kate quickly used the restroom, then returned to the concession stand and the youthful attendant. "Do you have that five-dollar bill?" she asked.

He held it up. Kate pulled a real bill from her handbag.

"I'll trade you," she said.

"Okay . . ." He eyed her as she stuffed the bill in a side pocket of her bag. "You're weird." He didn't say it in an unkind way; he was just stating the obvious.

Chapter Thirty-Four

"And now," the announcer said in his dramatic, even-paced voice, "dancing the Viennese waltz one more time—competitors Joe Tucker and Georgia Cline!"

The crowd erupted. Joe held a hand high as he led Georgia onto the floor. What was keeping Evelyn? She would hate missing her sister's performance. But Kate didn't see the blue-haired twin anywhere.

Hal had returned from wherever he'd gone. He was on the other side of his wife, quiet and watchful as always. Agent Norris had vanished.

Joe and Georgia pranced in a circle before coming to a halt in the center of the glossy hardwood floor. They struck their first pose as the audience quieted. Evelyn hadn't done a very good job with Georgia's hair, Kate thought. It was considerably flatter than it had been, as if the air had been let out of a balloon. Just how much hair spray had the woman used on the do before?

The music flowed across the floor, taking Georgia and Joe along with it in its one-two-three beat, Joe's cane keeping tempo. Kate had never seen the two dance with such soul. It was enticing, intimate almost. It was as if . . . Kate shook the thought from her head, then looked around to see where Evelyn had gone. Still no sight of her.

When the music finally faded, it was to a stunned audience. After a long moment of silence, wild clapping and cheering filled the room. Georgia blushed as she looked to Joe, who in turn motioned for her to take her bow. The crowd was on its feet then, spectators hooting and hollering as if they were at Fenway Park instead of a refined ballroom dance competition in Pine Ridge, Tennessee.

Joe grinned and waved at the crowd, then led Georgia off the floor. Kate exchanged a smile with Audrey, aware that she held the woman's counterfeit five-dollar bill in her handbag.

"They're actually going to win!" Audrey said. She shook her head and leaned to whisper something to her husband.

He smiled and kissed her on the cheek. Kate felt the counterfeit bill in the side compartment of her handbag. She hadn't had time to examine it.

Was it a fake as she'd suspected? It had to be. The soda machine had denied it even though it was as crisp and new as any bill fresh from the bank. Without magnetic ink, the fakes were easy to spot, assuming, that was, that the counterfeiter printed fresh bills on rag paper as well as bleaching real cash.

"AND NOW, THE WINNERS of the beginners' ballroom dance challenge . . ."

The voice that had been speaking to them all evening finally had a body. He was a scrawny man with sunken cheeks and a crew cut. As Kate looked at him, she couldn't reconcile the preconceived image she'd formed from his strong baritone voice with the reality of his puny physique.

Eight couples stood side by side as the man showboated in front of them center stage. "Give them a hand, everyone! Didn't they do a great job here tonight?"

The crowd obliged.

Georgia's dress looked a little baggy on her. Not much, but it no longer strained across her midriff.

She glanced around, looking for Evelyn. It wasn't like her not to be there watching the festivities. When Kate stretched, she thought she could make out the blue-haired twin just past the exit sign, but it was a faint glimpse.

"All right!" he went on, holding up an envelope. "In my hand I have the judges' decision."

He made a show of tearing the envelope open. A drumroll sounded as he read off the seventh- through the third-place finishers. Finally only Joe and Georgia remained, with a couple that looked to be in their early twenties.

"That leaves the husband-and-wife team of Christopher and Antoinette Mielke and partners Joe Tucker and Georgia Cline!"

As he said it, Evelyn took the seat next to Kate.

"Would he just get over it and announce the winner already?" Evelyn said.

Kate turned to look at her. Something about her didn't seem right.

"The winners of the two-thousand-dollar grand prize and the title of Grand Champions are"—he paused for dramatic effect—"Joe Tucker and Georgia Cline!"

Joe and Georgia waved to the crowd, while Evelyn sat back in her chair as if stunned.

Audrey was clapping furiously, while Hal and Paul offered more demure congratulations. Evelyn hadn't said a word, though her face was pale. Kate narrowed her eyes at her, studying the blue hair, the plain-looking outfit she'd changed into once she'd found out Fish wasn't coming.

The announcer said his farewells, and the crowd began to disperse.

"Mrs. Hanlon?" A man's voice pulled her attention. At first she didn't see him, since the lights behind him blinded her. Then she realized who it was—Agent Norris.

"I'm here to place you under arrest," he went on. "For conspiracy to counterfeit."

Kate's mouth dropped open, and Paul stood to protest.

"This is ridiculous!" he said. "There's no way on the planet that Kate is a counterfeiter."

"I'm sorry, Pastor Hanlon." The agent turned to him. "There was evidence at the storage facility—a camera with her fingerprints and shots of bills."

"That was planted, and you know it," Kate said, pointing a finger and rising to her feet.

The agent shook his head. "I have a young man here who is willing to testify that you exchanged money with him."

"But . . . but . . . ," Kate sputtered.

"Can I take a look in that side pocket of your handbag?" he said.

The young man nodded that that was where he'd seen her stash the money.

Kate couldn't believe it. Reluctantly she reached into

the pocket and handed it to him. There was no doubt that the money was counterfeit. He examined it, then handed it to Paul so he could have a look. Kate shot Audrey a look, but the woman had disappeared to the dance floor to congratulate her prize pupils.

"Let's not make a scene in the middle of this crowd," Agent Norris went on. "I'm here to take you to the Copper Mill jail."

KATE HAD PROTESTED riding in the backseat of the Secret Service agent's black sedan, insisting that they wait for a patrol car. But they hadn't been able to reach Sheriff Roberts.

"Should we add resisting arrest to your charges?" the agent said, staring her down.

Not even Paul could argue with that. So, reluctantly Kate got in. Paul promised that he'd keep trying to reach the sheriff and be right behind them in Kate's Honda.

As the car sped south out of town, Kate wondered if they were indeed heading to the jail in Copper Mill. Given her suspicions, who knew what the man was capable of? She stared out the window as the black Tennessee night pressed against the windows.

"You thought you were pretty smart, didn't you, Mrs. Hanlon?" the agent said, his eyes focused straight ahead.

"I don't know what you're talking about."

"All your snooping around. It's a great cover for your own part in this ring." His voice was condescending, almost gleeful.

"I'm no counterfeiter."

"How do you explain the bill in your handbag and the camera with your prints?"

"Maybe *you* should try to explain it." Kate saw his quick take in the mirror. She looked back to see if Paul was still following. His headlights shone from fifty or so feet back.

"I don't think you know who you're dealing with."

Fear came over Kate then. The tone of his voice, the menace in his words—she'd crossed some invisible line.

"So what do you want me to do, Agent Norris?" she said.

"First of all, stop your meddling. Counterfeiting is a serious crime, Mrs. Hanlon. It's the kind of thing people get *killed* over." The threat in his statement hung in the air between them. Kate's pulse quickened.

"How long have you and Mr. Harper been friends?" she ventured.

The agent seemed startled by the question. "What makes you think we're friends?"

"I've seen you together. I know more than you think. I know you were at the church the day the counterfeits were passed. I know you took things from the Lourdes' home to plant at the storage facility."

The man's eyes narrowed in the mirror at her.

"Hal and I worked together in Texas. That's all."

"So how did it work?" Kate said. "Hal made the counterfeits, and you were the guard dog, derailing any investigations that got too close to you by framing innocent bystanders? Tim was just an available scapegoat, isn't that right? How many other people have you sent to jail in your place, *Agent* Norris?"

She felt the car speed up. He turned right onto a gravel

road. Kate turned her head. Paul was there but farther back, losing ground to the racing sedan.

"And who is Max Lee?" she braved, realizing in that instant that she knew the answer to her own question. "You made him up, didn't you? It was all part of the frame—"

"You talk too much, Mrs. Hanlon."

Kate looked out the window. "Where are you taking me?"

The agent turned again, taking the first left. His driving had become erratic; he was all over the road, spitting gravel and dust as he flew.

"Agent Norris, this isn't the way to the Copper Mill jail. Why are you taking me on Hawk's Nest Road?"

The unmarked road was known by locals for the birds that lived there. She glanced back again. No sign of Paul.

"Keep your trap shut!" the agent snapped.

Chapter Thirty-Five

Kate pressed her back against the seat. Sweat beaded on her forehead. If the car hadn't been traveling so fast, she could have jumped out the door, but the road twisted and turned up the mountain, and steep drop-offs met the side rails closer to the top.

Agent Norris met her eyes in the rearview mirror. "Looks like we lost your husband," he said, cynical glee in his tone.

The blackness outside closed in. "Don't count on it."

Her ears popped, signaling that they neared the top of the mountain. She prayed for God to intervene, to give her wisdom, to rescue her, but when they came to a stop and the agent pulled her from the backseat, it seemed her prayers would go unanswered.

"You won't be interfering in other people's business anymore, lady." He squeezed her arm and dragged her across rocks and brambles toward the precipice.

"You're hurting me!" Kate cried. "They all saw you take me. How do you think you'll get away with this?"

"You'd be surprised how many things I've gotten away with," he hissed.

Her thoughts flew to Paul and their three children, to her grandchildren, then to Amy and Tim Lourdes and little Jake, who would be separated possibly forever if this man had his way.

"You can't do this!" she said, her voice echoing off the rocks.

"Just watch me!" He pulled her and held her by the shoulders, ready to send her plummeting to her death in the valley far below. "You can say good-bye, Mrs. Hanlon."

Just then, headlights illuminated them, and Kate took the moment of distraction to stomp on the man's foot, hard, with her high-heeled shoe. He let out a yowl of pain and loosened his grip. She fled toward the light, kicking her shoes off as she ran. Pain shot up her feet from the uneven, rocky ground.

Paul was there, followed within moments by a police car, its lights flashing. Agent Norris turned to run, but there was nowhere he could go except over the cliff. Finally he raised his hands over his head in surrender.

Sheriff Roberts handcuffed him and tugged him to the SUV as Kate and Paul held each other. Kate's body shook as the realization of what could have happened came to her. Paul stroked her hair and whispered softly into her ear. Finally he pulled back and looked into her eyes.

"You okay?" he said.

"Now I am." She smiled despite the stain of tears on her cheeks.

The sheriff was at their side. "Good thing you called 911,"

he said to Kate. He lifted his hat and scratched his head. "Deputy Spencer and reinforcements are on their way to the Harpers' as we speak. He'll give them the homecoming they deserve."

AMY LOURDES WAS AT HER DOOR at eight o'clock the next morning. "They're setting Tim free!" she said without even a hello. "Just like that, they're letting him go." Her pretty face glowed with excitement.

"Who's staying with Jake?" Kate said as Paul came to stand behind her in the doorway.

"My neighbor. She called a couple days ago to apologize and see if she could help with Jake." She looked from Kate to Paul, then winked. "So do you want to come with me to get Tim?"

Kate grinned. "Let me grab my handbag."

Tim was waiting for them in front of the town jail when Kate and Paul parked behind Amy's car. Though he looked too thin and pale, he smiled from ear to ear. Sheriff Roberts was with him, hat in hand as he spoke to the newly freed man. Amy flew out of the car and into his arms, practically knocking him over.

The sheriff met Kate's eyes with a nod and tucked his arms behind his back.

"You were right about everything. The Harpers had an elaborate counterfeiting operation in their garage," he said. "From what we can tell, they bleached sections of pre-1996 ones, fives and tens, and reprinted them at higher denominations so they still had characteristics of real money. They printed smaller counterfeit bills they figured people wouldn't bother checking, like that five you had. It was brilliant, really. From what we can estimate, they've passed over three hundred thousand dollars in fake bills across several states. Agent Wimper said that they're looking back at some of their prior cases to see who else the threesome framed."

"How can they just set up innocent people?" Kate asked, astounded by their lack of empathy for those they'd hurt.

The sheriff shook his head. "Near as we can tell with Tim Lourdes, the bank employee was an easy mark. He'd already taken some of the bills when he filled in at the teller counter, so they knew his prints were on them. Agent Norris—who seems to have been the guard dog of this operation—planted everything else after the fact."

"And the print shop at the storage facility?" Paul asked.

"Norris bribed the owner to say that Tim had rented it. The handwriting analysis would've borne that out, if Norris hadn't gotten his hands on the evidence and your camera."

Kate shook her head, disbelieving. "So Audrey was . . ."

"She was in on everything, Kate. The studio was part of their cover. All their possessions have been seized."

He looked Kate in the eye. "Thank you," he said sincerely. "It's a terrible thing what those people did to an innocent, hurting family. But the Lourdeses will soon be back together because of you."

JAKE'S COLOR HAD RETURNED along with the joy when he saw his father in his hospital room. His mouth dropped open, and he looked to his mother as if he wasn't sure he could believe his eyes.

"It's Daddy!" she confirmed.

"I'm free," Tim said, pulling his son into an embrace.

Jake coughed deep in his chest, though his smile never dimmed. He closed his eyes, and the taut lines of his face relaxed for the first time in a long time.

"I was so worried for Mommy," he said. "She needs us."

Tim pulled back and gazed into his son's serious face.

"She does need us." He winked at Amy as tears streamed down her cheeks. "And you need to get healthy." He held his son for a long time.

Kate couldn't help but tear up at the sight.

Finally Tim stood, ruffling his son's hair as he did. Then he turned to Kate and held out a hand. "We can't thank you enough, Kate."

Kate took his hand in a warm grasp.

"What will you do now?" she asked.

"The bank has offered me my job back, and I'll stay for a little bit until Jake's out of the hospital. But we'd really like to take him to that cystic fibrosis facility in Memphis." He looked at his wife. "Since Amy's family is there, we're going to head home, job or not, and trust God for the rest."

Amy grinned. "My sister said we can live with her and her husband until we get on our feet."

Kate turned her eyes to Jake. "How do you feel about that?"

His dark-rimmed eyes smiled, belying his tired body. "I'm just happy to have my daddy back."

Epilogue

The big moving truck parked in front of the Lourdes' home seemed so final to Kate. She would miss this devoted family when they were gone. That morning the church had presented them with the offering they'd taken all those months before, and Tim had gratefully accepted.

Jake's health prognosis had improved dramatically since the lung transplant. He no longer made that rattling sound when he breathed. It didn't mean his cystic fibrosis was cured, but it did mean he had time to grow into a man and live a full life. Perhaps a cure would be found.

"He's in the hands of God," Amy told Kate as they watched the boy say a tearful farewell to his friends, their skinny bodies hugging.

Tim was at her side, looking like his old Beach Boys self.

"That's the only place to be," Kate said, touching the younger woman's arm in a motherly way.

They watched as the moving company brought out piece after piece of furniture and carefully placed them in the truck, like putting together a jigsaw puzzle they'd completed many times before.

"We . . . uh . . ." A voice behind them drew their attention. It was Joe Tucker and one of the Cline sisters. They both wore sheepish expressions.

Joe looked at Amy, then at Jake.

Amy and Tim turned toward them, curious. Joe lifted his face and said, "You probably heard about that dance contest we won."

Tim nodded.

"We both agreed that we didn't want to do it just to look good," Joe kept going. "Or for selfish gain. I mean, what would be the purpose in that?"

"Joe and I don't have anything that we need at our ages," the blue-haired senior put in, "and we know how hard these times must be for you, especially with—"

Joe held up a finger, silencing the woman.

"We wanted you to have this." He handed Tim an envelope.

Tim seemed shocked at first. He looked at Amy, then at Kate.

"Well, open it," Joe insisted.

Tim slid his finger inside the flap and pulled out two checks for one thousand dollars each. "We can't accept thi—"

"You sure can accept it," Joe said. "It was part of the reason I agreed to do the competition. I told you about my niece's little girl," he went on. "I know what it's like to love someone with that ailment. And when Georgia told me that there was a cash prize, I saw it as an opportunity."

Tim handed the gift to Amy.

"How can we thank you?" Amy said.

"You just did," Joe said.

Amy pulled the elderly woman into an embrace. The woman smiled, and a tear escaped her lashes.

Kate gave the Cline twin a wink. She'd *thought* something hadn't been quite right at the competition—the soulfulness of the dance, the loose fit of the clothes, the flat hair, Evelyn missing out on the competition . . . It all served to confirm Kate's suspicions.

Evelyn had taken Georgia's place in the dance final.

Kate smiled at the blue-haired twin. If Evelyn wanted to keep the switch a secret, then Kate would respect that.

"Sounds like cause for celebration," Paul said.

"You'll have to celebrate without us." Tim pointed to the van, which was now full. The movers closed the back door. "We're on our way!"

As the Lourdes waved good-bye, Kate glanced at her husband, then at Joe and Evelyn.

She realized that the best deeds were those done with no thought for self, but from a heart for those in need.

About the Author

BEFORE LAUNCHING her writing career, Traci DePree worked as a fiction editor for many of the best Christian authors in the country. While still maintaining her editing career, Traci loves making up new worlds in her novels. Her hope is that, just as in Copper Mill, Tennessee, her readers will see God's creation and inspiration within the people in their own lives. Traci is the author of the best-selling Lake Emily series, including *A Can of Peas*, *Dandelions in a Jelly Jar* and *Aprons on a Clothesline*. She makes her home in a small Minnesota town with her husband and their five children, the youngest joining the family via adoption.

A Note from the Editors

THIS ORIGINAL BOOK was created by the Books and Inspirational Media Division of Guideposts, the world's leading inspirational publisher. Founded in 1945 by Dr. Norman Vincent Peale and Ruth Stafford Peale, Guideposts helps people from all walks of life achieve their maximum personal and spiritual potential. Guideposts is committed to communicating positive, faith-filled principles for people everywhere to use in successful daily living.

Our publications include award-winning magazines such as *Guideposts* and *Angels on Earth*, best-selling books, and outreach services that demonstrate what can happen when faith and positive thinking are applied in day-to-day life.

For more information, visit us at www.guideposts.com, call (800) 431-2344 or write Guideposts, PO Box 5815, Harlan, Iowa 51593.